MELVIN BEEDERMAN SUPERHERO

MELVIN BEEDERMAN SUPERHERO

THE GRATEFUL FRED

GREG TRINE

ILLUSTRATED BY
RHODE MONTIJO

HENRY HOLT AND COMPANY ★ NEW YORK

To Mom and Dad
—G. T.

For my brother Alex
—R. M.

Henry Holt and Company, LLC
Publishers since 1866
175 Fifth Avenue, New York, New York 10010
www.henryholtchildrensbooks.com

Henry Holt® is a registered trademark of Henry Holt and Company, LLC.
Text copyright © 2006 by Greg Trine
Illustrations copyright © 2006 by Rhode Montijo
All rights reserved. Distributed in Canada by H. B. Fenn and Company Ltd.

Library of Congress Cataloging-in-Publication Data
Trine, Greg.
The Grateful Fred / Greg Trine ;
illustrated by Rhode Montijo.—1st hardcover and pbk. eds.
p.   cm.—(Melvin Beederman, superhero)
Summary: When the star of The Grateful Fred receives threatening letters,
he calls on Melvin, the superhero in charge of Los Angeles,
and his assistant, Candace, to stop the criminal and his henchmen
before they destroy Fred's reputation.
ISBN-13: 978-0-8050-7921-0 / ISBN-10: 0-8050-7921-1 (hardcover)
1   3   5   7   9   10   8   6   4   2

ISBN-13: 978-0-8050-7922-7 / ISBN-10: 0-8050-7922-X (paperback)
1   3   5   7   9   10   8   6   4   2

[1. Heroes—Fiction.   2. Musicians—Fiction.   3. Rock and roll music—Fiction.
4. Los Angeles (Calif.)—Fiction.   5. Humorous stories.]
I. Montijo, Rhode, ill.   II. Title.   III. Series.
PZ7.T7356Gra 2006   [Fic]—dc22   2005036322

First Edition—2006
Hand-lettering by David Gatti
Book designed by Laurent Linn
Printed in the United States of America on acid-free paper. ∞

CONTENTS

THE SUPERHERO'S LAB

Superhero Melvin Beederman was in his tree house taking it easy. Well, sort of. At least he wasn't chasing bad guys. The McNasty Brothers were once again in prison, and so Melvin decided it was time to invent the world's best-tasting ice cream. After all, it was an unwritten part of the Superhero's Code to eat snacks when they weren't saving the world.

So ice cream it was. And not just any ice cream—pretzel-flavored ice cream. Melvin had converted his tree house, which usually served as his good guy hideout, into a superhero's laboratory. All around him were sacks of sugar and cartons of milk.

Let's see, Melvin said to himself, *68 cups of sugar, 111 cups of milk. That's 179 cups in all.*

Ah . . . math. When Melvin wasn't saving the world or pounding on bad guys, there was always a good math problem just waiting to be solved.

He mixed up a big batch of pretzel-flavored ice cream and spooned some for his pet, Hugo. Hugo was a rat, but right now he was a guinea pig.

The rat licked his lips. He twitched his whiskers.

"*Squeakity-squeak squeak?*" Melvin asked Hugo. This either meant, "How does it taste?" or possibly, "Does your belly button itch?" Melvin had once been fluent in gerbil, but he wasn't so sure about rat.

"*Squeak,*" the rat said. This either meant, "This is the best ice cream ever," or "Don't quit your day job, mister."

No problem there. Years ago, Melvin had been plucked from an orphanage and sent to the Superhero Academy. He was now the superhero in charge of Los

Angeles. With his superhero assistant, Candace Brinkwater, he kept the peace. No, he wouldn't be giving up his day job, not as long as his town needed him.

Melvin looked around his hideout-turned-inventor's-lab and cleaned up. He wasn't giving up on pretzel-flavored ice cream, but he had things to do. After cleaning up, he checked his e-mail.

From: grateful@fred.fred
To: melvin@melvinbeederman.com

Dear Melvin,
We need your help. Someone has been sending us threatening letters. We don't know who it is. Please come to our concert tonight, just in case.
Sincerely,
Fred of The Grateful Fred

"Holy trouble-is-brewing!" Melvin said. "Someone is out to get The Grateful Fred. I love those guys."

Holy trouble-is-brewing, indeed! He *did* love them. The Grateful Fred was his all-time favorite rock-and-roll band. Melvin had to get going. The e-mail was a cry for help, and the Superhero's Code told him what to do in such situations. Melvin knew he had to be at the concert. He had to keep the peace. And if he could do it *and* listen to great tunes, all the better.

He turned on the TV so Hugo could watch *The Adventures of Thunderman*, their favorite show. Thunderman and his assistant, Thunder Thighs, were the second-best superheroes Melvin knew.

"Gotta go, Hugo," he said as he dove out the window and—

5

Crash!

Melvin hardly ever got off the ground in one try. He stood and tried again. "Up, up, and away."

Splat!

"Up, up, and away."

Thud!

"Up, up, and away."

Kabonk!

Finally he was up and flying—on the fifth try. This was par for the course for Melvin Beederman. At least he was flying.

Now if only he could learn how to turn off his x-ray vision. He really hated seeing everyone's underwear. But as he zoomed between the tall buildings of Los Angeles, looking down at the people, that's what he saw—underwear.

All over the place. In every shape, color, and size. It was nauseating, really. He had to remind himself not to eat before going to work.

ROCK AND ROLLER'S CODE:
SAY "BABY" AND "YEAH" A LOT

Melvin zoomed across town, trying to ignore the underwear. He couldn't wait to hear his favorite band, The Grateful Fred. They had fans all over the world. They were more popular than U2. They had more gold albums than Me3. They rocked harder than Us4.

The Grateful Fred knew the Rock and Roller's Code, and this was one of the reasons for their success. Their first album was called *Yeah, Yeah, Baby*.

Their second album was called *Baby, Baby, Yeah*. And their third was called *Baby, Yeah, Baby*.

Yes, the Rock and Roller's Code was working just fine.

Melvin arrived at the concert just as the first song was starting. He hovered above the crowd, which was going wild, as Fred, the leader of The Grateful Fred, sang their latest hit—
"Baby, Yeah, Yeah."

Melvin watched the crowd for any sign of foul play. He had a nose for such things. It was his nose that helped him catch the McNasty Brothers, who, as everyone knows, smelled worse than rotting Brussels sprouts.

Melvin circled above the concert. He saw no sign of danger, no sign that anything bad was about to happen. The Fredheads—this is what the fans called themselves—were too busy having fun to think devious thoughts, let alone sinister ones. And so Melvin relaxed and enjoyed the concert.

Big mistake!

Suddenly an explosion ripped through the air—KABOOM! The stage began to collapse. The Fredheads screamed and scattered in all directions.

"Holy stampede!" Melvin said. "This is terrible."

Holy stampede, indeed! It *was* terrible. The stage crumbled, falling toward the crowd. People were about to be crushed. Melvin shot out of the sky to the rescue. He got there just in time. Just in the nick of time, in fact. He grabbed the stage and held it up until all those near it got clear and The Grateful Fred band members climbed down.

"How can I ever thank you?" Fred said.

"Just doing my job," Melvin replied, which, of course, was part of the Superhero's Code. And Melvin always kept to the code.

Fred unstrapped himself from his guitar. "I can't understand it. Who would do such a thing?"

"Not sure," Melvin said. "But I'm going to find out." He walked behind the stage where no one could see him and took off.

Or at least he tried to.

"Up, up, and away."

Crash!

Splat!

Thud!

Kabonk!

Once again, Melvin was up and flying on the fifth try. But he couldn't think about his flying problems right now. Someone was out to get The Grateful Fred, and he had to find out who. And why.

He knew he couldn't solve this one alone. He needed help. He needed his assistant, Candace Brinkwater. The only person ever to score 500 points in a basketball game. The only person to run the hundred-yard dash in three and a half seconds. The only third-grader who could fly.

HARK!

Melvin flew between the tall buildings of Los Angeles. The moon was out and he could see his reflection in the glass. He hovered and flexed, then continued on. Flexing was not part of the Superhero's Code. It was just a Melvin thing.

He tumbled to a stop on Candace's front lawn, then went around back and threw a few pebbles at her bedroom window. He had once seen Romeo do this in the play *Romeo and Juliet*.

Candace opened the window and looked out.

"Hark!" Melvin said.

"What?"

"Oh, sorry, wrong story. Candace, I need your help."

"You know I can't save the world after dinnertime," she said. And it was way beyond dinnertime. Candace was in her pajamas.

"Get your cape and let's go," Melvin said. "If we wait till tomorrow the trail will be cold and we'll never catch him."

"Catch who?"

"Someone is trying to kill The Grateful Fred!"

Candace looked shocked. She began to hum the melody of "Baby, Yeah, Yeah."

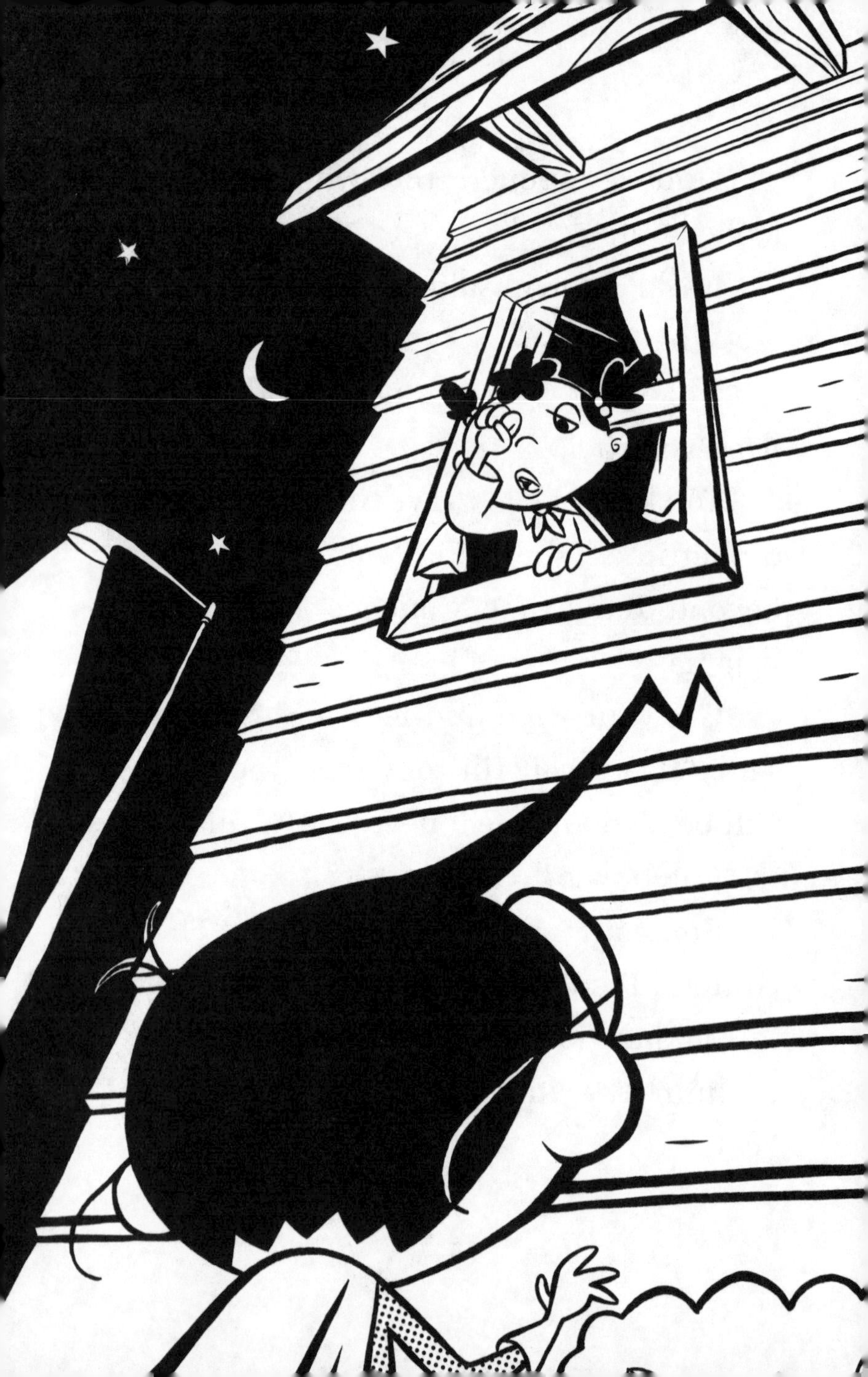

Then she caught herself and said, "I love those guys."

"Well, someone doesn't. We have to find whoever it is before they try it again."

"Meet me after school at the library," Candace said. "Don't you worry, Melvin Beederman. We'll catch him, right after we do my math homework."

This was their agreement. Melvin helped Candace with math, and she helped him save the world . . . one bad guy at a time.

Candace closed the window and disappeared behind the curtains, leaving Melvin alone in the backyard. Should he go off and try to find the bad guy tonight? Melvin thought this over, then shook his head. No, he was part of a team. He'd wait until his partner in uncrime could join him.

"Up, up, and away."

Crash!

Splat!

Thud!

Kabonk!

Melvin flew home to his tree house. Hugo the rat was there waiting for him.

"*Squeaker squeakity?*" Hugo said.

"*Squeak,*" Melvin replied. He didn't feel like talking. Or squeaking, for that matter.

JOE THE BAD GUY

The Grateful Fred may have been one of the best rock-and-roll bands in the world. They may have sold more records than U2, Me3, and Us4 combined. But that didn't mean everyone in the world loved them.

In fact, there was one guy who hated them. This was Joe the Bad Guy. He used to be Joe the Okay Guy. Before that he was Joe the Semi-Nice Guy. But now he was just plain Bad. And he was rapidly heading toward Dreadful.

He hated The Grateful Fred. And now he hated Melvin Beederman.

"Darn you, Melvin Beederman," Joe the Bad Guy said. He had placed the bomb beneath the stage at the concert and was now pacing back and forth in his lair. Not hideout—lair.

Actually, it wasn't *his* lair. He had only recently made the jump from Okay Guy to Bad Guy and so he was just renting.

He went to Big Al's Rent-a-Lair and got a deal on a used one. Still, a lair was a lair. And it was a good place to come up with more devious and sinister plans.

Should he be sinister today or should he be devious? It was a toss-up, really. Joe the Bad Guy couldn't decide. He had been devious on Monday and Wednesday, and sinister on Tuesday and Thursday. It seemed he could go either way, since now it was Friday.

All he knew was that he just had to get The Grateful Fred. And if Melvin Beederman got in the way, Joe would get him, too.

Joe sat down in his lair (it came furnished) and thought about the days when he had been in The Grateful Fred.

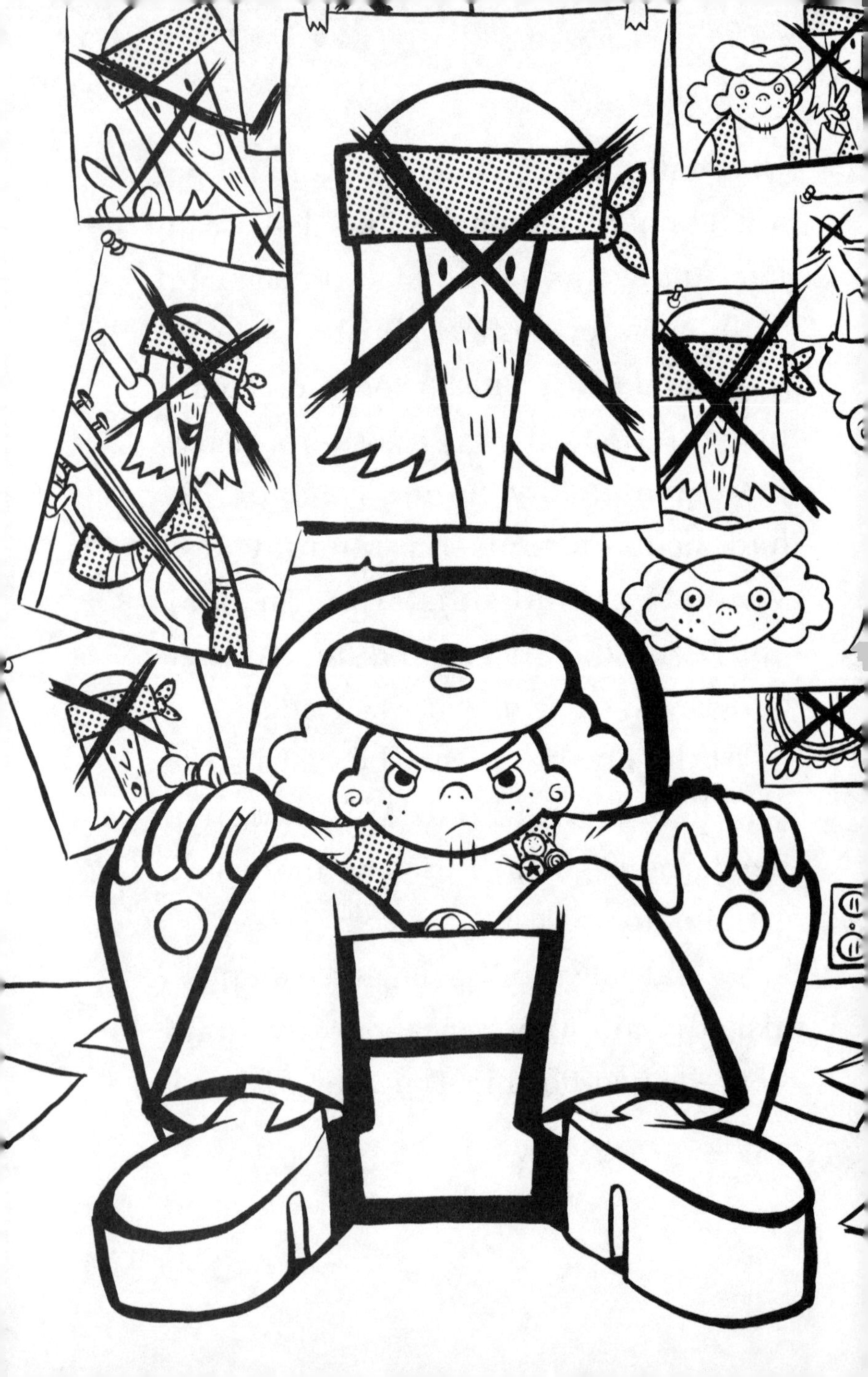

He had been kicked out by Fred himself, the band's leader. And now all Joe could think about was getting revenge.

Fred had kicked him out for one big reason: Joe was a terrible musician. But it wasn't entirely his fault. He came from a long line of terrible musicians. His dad was terrible. So was his mother. Even his goldfish had no rhythm at all. Joe had once put a tiny drum set in the bottom of the aquarium, and that fish could not keep a beat if his life depended on it. Of course, he couldn't hold the drumsticks either.

The more successful The Grateful Fred became, the more Joe hated them. One way or another he'd get his revenge.

Joe looked out the window of his lair. "One way or another," he said.

THE FREDS

The question was: how to get revenge? He'd already tried once and Melvin Beederman had come to save the day. It was enough to make any bad guy want to throw up.

What to do? Joe wondered. It was a well-known fact that not only was Melvin Beederman a serious Grateful Fred fan, but he also had brains—noggin power. Joe never made it past sixth grade. How do you beat a smart guy who can bench press a Buick? How do you defeat a guy who can fly? Was it wise to mess with someone who can see your underwear? Joe didn't have the answers. He just knew he had to try.

And so he spent the night thinking of his next move. He paced. He drank tons of coffee. He even watched a little of *The Adventures of Thunderman*. He wasn't a big fan of Thunderman . . . or Thunder Thighs. He just wanted to pick up any tips he could. Thunderman was a super-hero. How did the bad guys on the show deal with him?

The answer to Joe's problem was to get help, of course. If he didn't have much in the brain department, he'd find someone who did. When morning came, he headed off to see the only guy who could possibly have what he was looking for—Big Al.

Not only did Big Al rent lairs at Rent-a-Lair, he also sold bad-guy stuff. Big Al's motto was *Serving Southern California's Bad Guys Since 1985*. If anyone could solve Joe's problem with The Grateful Fred, Al could.

"I have to get revenge on my enemy, Al. Any suggestions?"

Al stroked his chin. "Ah . . . revenge. A worthy cause. Are you sure I can't interest you in a new lair? Look at this baby, comes with an indoor Jacuzzi."

"I already have a lair. What do you have in the way of gadgets? In the destroy-your-enemy department?"

"We're having a sale on time bombs. Buy one, get one free." Al gestured to a large stack of bombs. "They even come in a variety of colors—orange, green, and blue."

Joe thought about this. He had already tried a bomb, but Melvin showed up just in the nick of time.

Joe shook his head. "What else do you have?"

"Not in the mood to blow someone up, eh?"

"Not really."

"Well, you can always frame him," Al suggested. "You know, make your enemy look bad, then let the police make his life miserable."

Al was too brilliant for words! This was the idea Joe was looking for.

Al took him into his office and closed the door. He pointed to a box across the room. "The Clone-o-Matic 6000, by Acme."

"Acme?" Joe was confused. "The bologna company?"

"Acme's into everything. They do more than bologna."

Al gave Joe a big discount on the cloning machine. After all, Joe was a faithful customer. And there wasn't a lot of that going around in the bad-guy

community. There also wasn't a big
demand for cloning your enemies.

Joe could hardly wait to
get back to his lair
and clone a Fred.
Or two.

MEANWHILE ...

While Joe the Bad Guy was home in his lair making plans to ruin Fred's life, Melvin Beederman was getting ready to head off to the library to meet with his partner in uncrime, Candace Brinkwater.

Before he did, he turned on the TV so Hugo the rat could watch *The Adventures of Thunderman* (and Thunder Thighs) while he was gone.

"Squeak squeakity," Melvin said. This

either meant, "Have a great day, young rodent," or "Have you ever thought about taking up the trombone in your spare time?" Rat talk was very difficult sometimes.

Melvin threw himself out the window. He knew he'd be able to fly on the first try, one of these days.

This was not one of those days.

Crash!

On the fifth try, he was up and flying. As usual. This is getting old, he said to himself as he zoomed across town. Looking down, he saw the people of Los Angeles in their underwear. That was getting even older.

Melvin Beederman arrived at the library just as his partner in uncrime did. Candace Brinkwater took out her math book, and the two of them got to work.

When they finished her math home-work, Candace said, "Now, what's this about The Grateful Fred?"

"Someone's out to get them," Melvin said, quickly looking away as the ancient librarian walked by.

"What's wrong?" Candace asked. "You look like you're about to throw up."

"I am. I just saw the librarian's underwear."

Somehow Candace had learned to turn off her x-ray vision. Melvin had not. Candace could also get up in the air on the first try, while Melvin still struggled with it.

"We need to find out who it is before he strikes again," Melvin said. "Who knows every bad guy in town?"

Candace thought this over. "Big Al?"

"Exactly. He's been serving Southern California's bad guys since 1985. If anyone knows something, he does."

They went outside and Candace launched herself. Melvin joined her. Or tried to.

Crash!

Splat!

Thud!

Kabonk!

On the fifth try he joined her where she had been hovering above the trees. Then they flew off to Big Al's Rent-a-Lair. Melvin paused only once to flex along the way. When he was on an important mission he kept his flexing to a bare minimum.

Al was out in front of his store when Melvin and Candace touched down. "Can I interest you in a lair?" Al asked, faking a big smile. He crossed his arms over his enormous belly.

"We're good guys," Melvin said. "Notice the capes and boots."

"Call it a hideout then. Every good guy needs a hideout. We even have one with a Jacuzzi."

"We're looking for someone who may be a customer of yours," Melvin said.

Big Al smirked. "You and every other crime fighter in town."

"Someone is out to get The Grateful Fred. Do you have any ideas who that might be?"

Al began humming "Baby, Yeah, Baby, Baby." Then he caught himself and said, "The Grateful Fred? I love those guys. Who would want to hurt them?"

"We'd like to ask you that same question," Candace spoke up. She usually let Melvin do the talking, since he had better noggin power, but that was getting very boring.

"Sorry," Al said. "No can do. If word got around that I was snitching on my customers I'd be out of business. Bad guys would hate me. You know, I've been serving Southern California's bad guys since 1985."

Melvin turned to leave. He knew there was no use arguing. Al was not going to let his business go down the tubes, even if it meant saving The Grateful Fred. But Melvin also knew that Al had information that he needed. He wondered what the Superhero's Code said about breaking and entering.

"What do we do now?" Candace asked.

"I have a plan," Melvin said. "But it may involve doing some night work. How do you feel about that?"

This was a tough one. Candace was all for saving the world, as long as she was home for dinner. But she also loved The Grateful Fred. Maybe some things were more important than following the rules.

"Anything for The Grateful Fred," she said finally and launched herself in the air.

"I'll come and get you at midnight," Melvin called to her. "Bring a flashlight, Candace."

He decided to jog home rather than try to launch himself in public.

THE CLONE-O-MATIC 6000

The Grateful Fred's latest tune, "Baby, Yeah, Baby, Baby," was number four on the hit charts. And climbing. Every time it moved up, Joe the Bad Guy got madder.

What did he do when he got mad? Punch something, that's what—usually the walls of his lair. You could always tell when The Grateful Fred had a hit song by the hundreds of dents in Joe's walls.

He had tried to go solo after he was kicked out of the band, but no one liked his music. They hated his lyrics even more. His song "You Have Hairy Knuckles but I Love You Anyhow" was turned down by every record company in the country. His song "Bucktoothed Sally" did even worse. A record company in England said they'd pay him to burn his music equipment. Once he played for free at a wedding reception, but after just one song everyone left the party and went bowling. Poor Joe the Bad Guy. He couldn't even work for free.

And so with every Grateful Fred hit song, his hatred deepened. He wanted revenge and he wanted it now. Sooner if possible!

Back in his lair, Joe began putting the Clone-o-Matic 6000 together. The Grateful Fred would soon pay the price

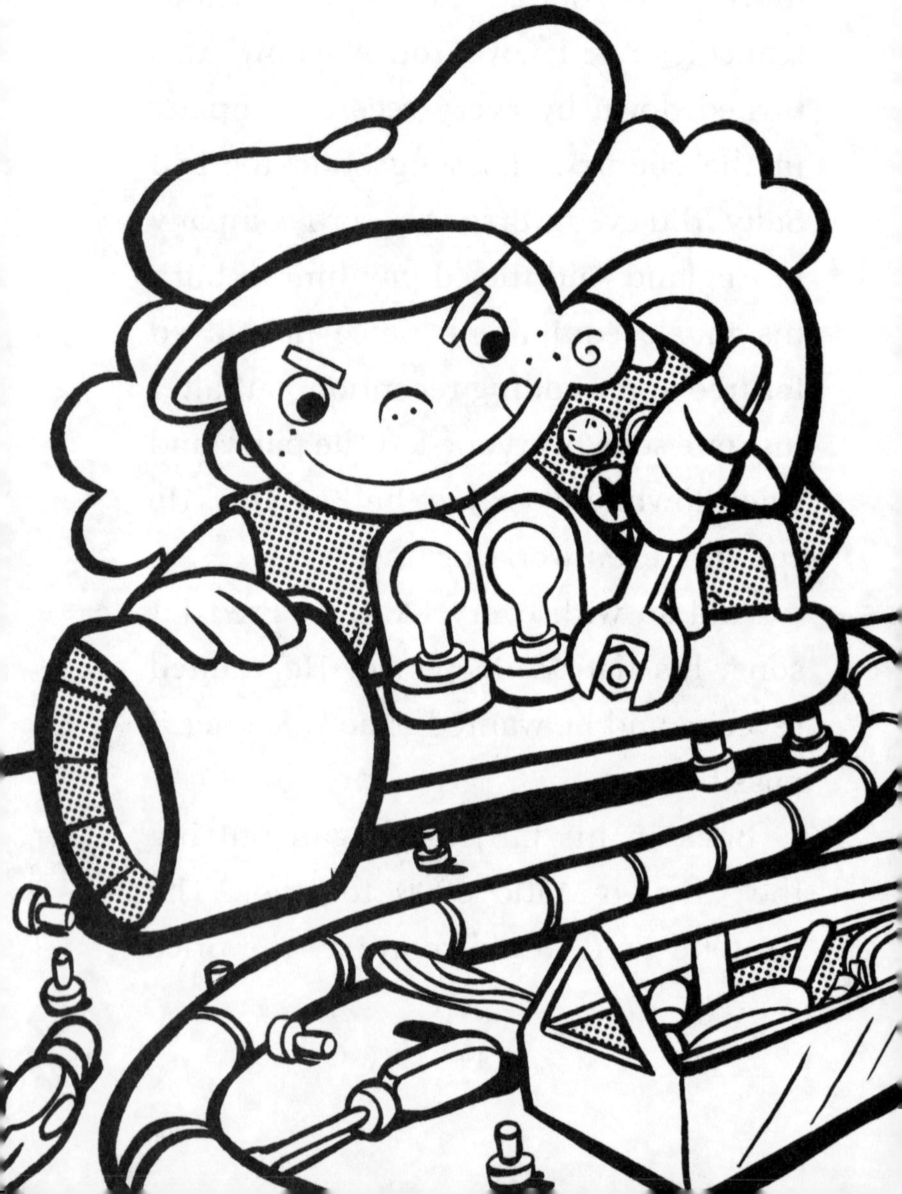

for kicking him out, he thought with an evil laugh. His evil laugh wasn't quite what it should be, but he planned to read up on the subject. He'd gotten a copy of *Perfecting Your Evil Laugh* at Big Al's and was going to start reading it as soon as he took care of The Grateful Fred.

But there was a problem. In order to clone a person, you needed to start with a piece of that person. You couldn't create something from nothing.

He needed a piece of Fred. A strand of hair. A toenail clipping.

At the stroke of midnight, Joe set out to get the piece of Fred that he needed.

SPEAKING OF MIDNIGHT

Melvin looked up at Candace's bedroom window. He waited until midnight before tossing the first pebble.

"Hark!" he said when she appeared.

"Wrong story again," she said. She climbed out of the window and joined him. Then the two of them took off. Or at least Candace did.

Crash!

Splat!

"Hurry up, Melvin," Candace called, hovering above the trees.

Yes, Melvin, would you get a move on? You're holding up the story.

"Who said that?" Candace asked.

"Who said what?" Melvin said, launching himself on the fifth try.

"Who said, 'You're holding up the story'?"

"Some handsome genius."

"Who?"

"The narrator. Don't encourage him." Melvin zoomed off toward Big Al's Rent-a-Lair. Candace stayed with him. "Can I kick in the door?" she asked.

Melvin had kicked in the last door. They usually took turns at this, since kicking in doors was a big superhero perk.

"I'm going to try my hand at picking the lock," Melvin said. "I don't want Al to know anyone has been here."

Melvin and Candace snuck around to the lot behind the store. They were surrounded by lairs.

"Look at this," Candace said. "A lair with a Jacuzzi."

"You're one of the good guys. You don't need a lair."

"But I've never had a lair. Can I have a lair, Melvin? Please, can I?"

Melvin put a finger to his lips. "Shhh!"

"At least you have a hideout. All I have is a stupid bedroom."

"WOULD YOU BE QUIET!" Melvin had removed a stiff wire from his pocket and grabbed the doorknob. It was unlocked.

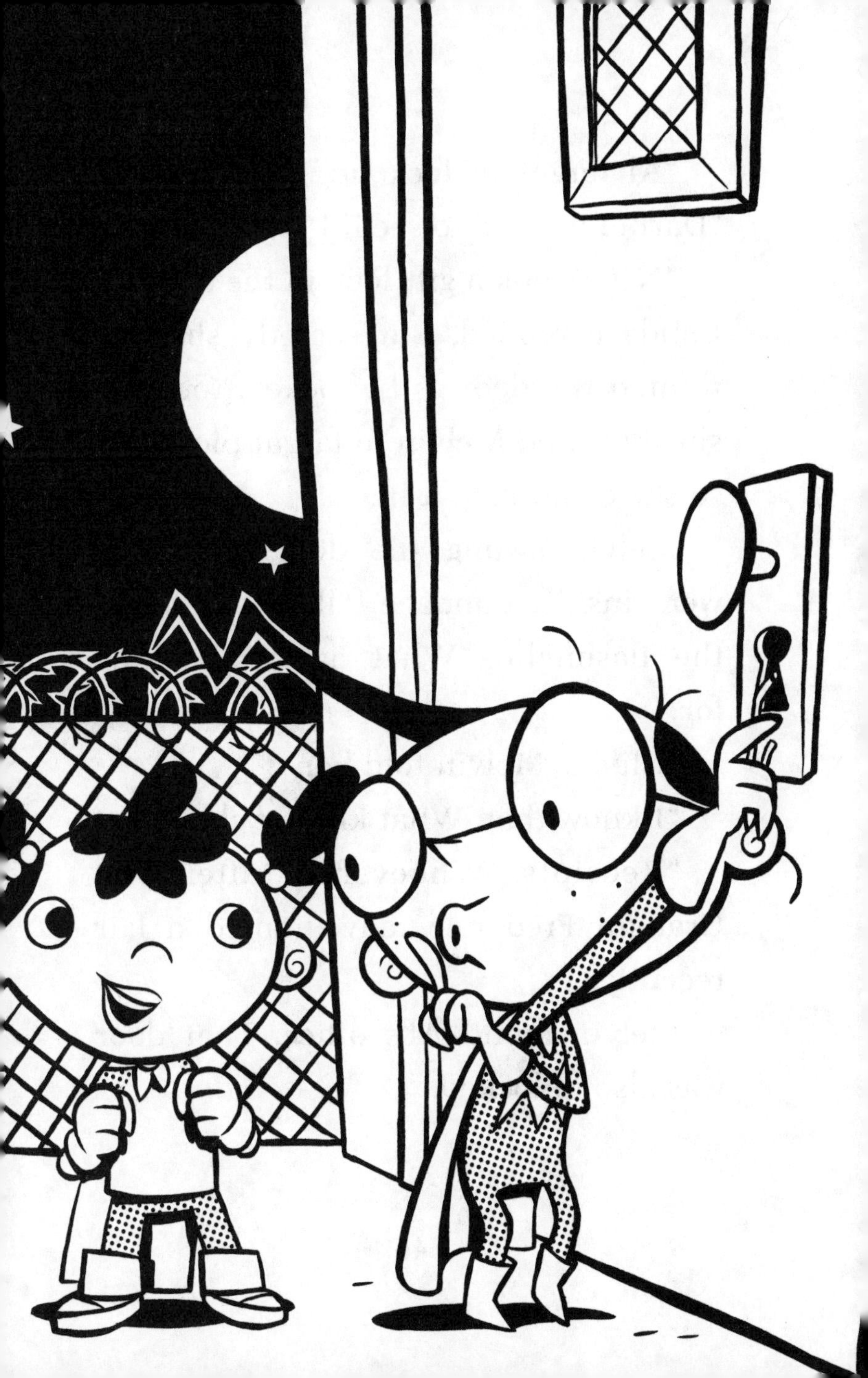

"Al forgot to lock up," Melvin said. "Darn! I wanted to see if I could pick it."

"Never look a gift-lock in the mouth," Candace replied. But secretly she had wanted the door to be locked, too, and she'd wanted Melvin to fail at picking it so she could kick it in.

Melvin swung the door open and went inside. Candace followed, holding the flashlight. "What are we looking for?"

"Clues," Melvin told her.

"I know that. What kind of clues?"

"Receipts. Whoever is after The Grateful Fred may have rented a lair recently."

Melvin found Al's office. That door was also unlocked.

"Darn," Candace said under her breath.

Melvin started going through a filing cabinet. "Uh-oh," he said. "They had a storewide lair sale last week. They sold a dozen lairs." Melvin read the sales receipts out loud. "Max the Wonder Thug, Stinky Gillespie, Calamity Wayne. Hey, the McNasty Sisters are in here."

"So what do we do?"

"We go down the list. See who has a grudge against The Grateful Fred. See who doesn't have an alibi for the night of the concert."

"I don't suppose we could find a door to kick in before we go?" Candace asked. "I'm kind of going through withdrawal."

"We don't have time," Melvin said,

stuffing the list in his pocket. "On the next case I'll let you kick in two doors. How does that sound?"

"That sounds—"

Suddenly something growled at them from the darkness outside the office. Candace swung the flashlight beam and there in the doorway was—

Please
stand By:

The Narrator Is on
a Coffee Break

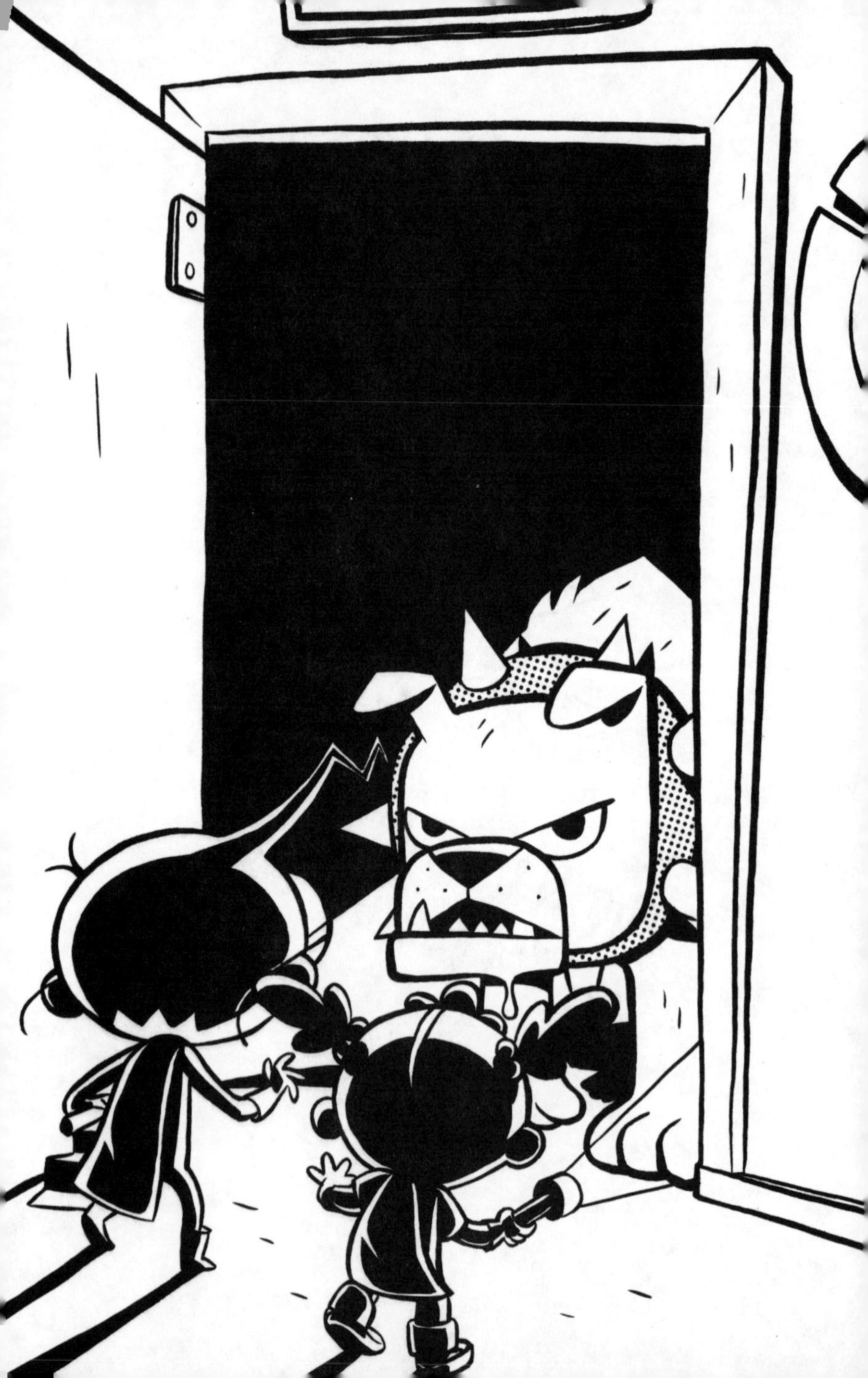

—the biggest dog she had ever seen.

"Holy Rottweiler!" Candace said. She backed up into the office.

Holy Rottweiler, indeed! It *was* the biggest one they'd ever seen.

And the meanest looking.

Meaner than a school principal on a bad day . . .

Meaner than the McNasty brothers . . .

Meaner than a junkyard dog.

Hey, that sounds like a song.

The dog drooled a lot too—like it was going out of style. Melvin and Candace backed farther into the room.

"What's the plan, Melvin? We need noggin power and we need it now!"

The dog growled again and moved toward them.

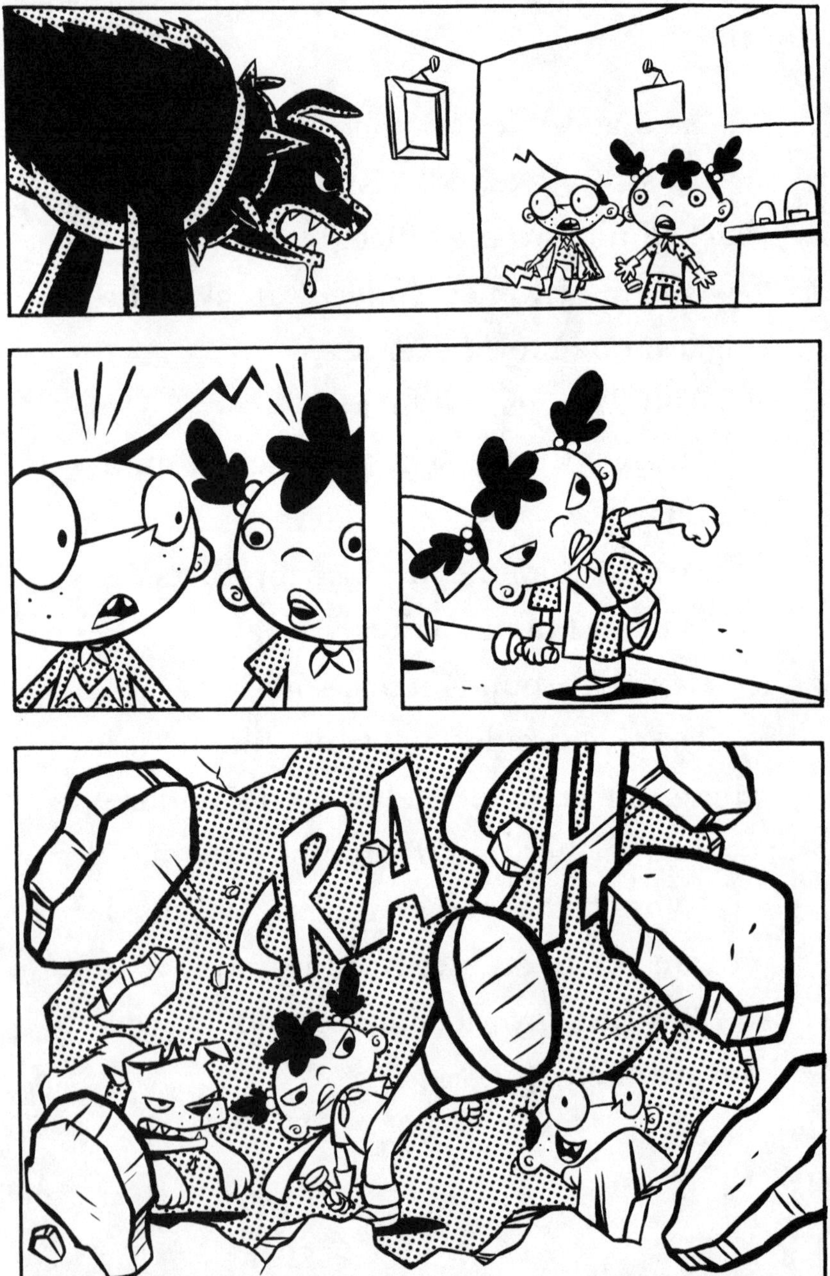
CRASH

"Melvin?" Candace said in a very unsuperhero voice.

"How do you feel about kicking in a wall?" Melvin said. "It's our only way out. Go for it, Candace."

Candace didn't need to be told twice. She kicked through the wall and Melvin followed her out. They found themselves in the back lot of Rent-a-Lair, the dog hot on their tail.

"In there," Melvin said, pointing to the lair with the Jacuzzi.

They ran inside and slammed the door just ahead of the dog. Candace flashed her light around. "I'm asking for a raise in my allowance. I gotta get one of these."

JOE THE BAD GUY'S
MIDNIGHT RUN

It was just after midnight when Joe the Bad Guy set off for the Hollywood Hills. This was where Fred of The Grateful Fred lived. It wasn't part of the Rock and Roller's Code to live in a mansion on a hill, but it was very common.

Joe made his way through the back gate of Fred's house, past the pool and Jacuzzi, and began checking doors and windows. All the doors were locked, but he found an open bathroom window and climbed through. Now to find Fred, he said to himself, grabbing the toenail clippers out of his pocket. He moved through the dark hallways and rooms humming "Yeah, Yeah, Baby, Baby." He hated The Grateful Fred but he couldn't get their music out of his head.

He didn't find Fred right away. But he did find his music equipment. Fred had a large collection of electric guitars in his den. And Joe set about cutting the strings—he had the clippers to do the job. *Just in case the clone idea doesn't work,* Joe said to himself. Besides, it was always a good idea to destroy your enemy's guitars. It simply made sense. This wasn't part of the Bad Guy's Code, but it sure felt right to Joe.

Once he'd finished, he looked around

at the guitars with the broken strings and kissed the toenail clippers before returning them to his pocket. *This was an ideal time to use his evil laugh,* he thought. But of course he hadn't perfected it yet. And he didn't want to wake up Fred, wherever he was. He'd laugh later, he decided, when he finished the job.

Where was Fred? That was the big question. Maybe the band was on tour, or maybe Fred was on vacation. Joe went from door to door in the darkened house—bathrooms, bedrooms, closets. But no Fred. Joe was beginning to get worried. With no Fred, there was no evil plan, and with no evil plan, there would be no revenge. And with no revenge we would have one sad bad guy on our hands, and we just can't have that, can we?

"No, we can't," Joe whispered.

I wasn't talking to you.

"Oh."

Joe went through all the rooms on the second floor, then headed to the kitchen. All this bad-guy work was making him hungry. Unlike superheroes, who like to snack when they're not working, bad guys like to snack while they're working. It's one of the major differences between good guys and bad guys. Also, bad guys smell worse. In Joe's case, a lot worse.

Fred was asleep on the living room couch, surrounded by root beer and pizza. It wasn't part of the Rock and Roller's Code to party all the time, but that was also very common.

Joe forgot his hunger as soon as he saw Fred. He tiptoed over and snipped

off a chunk of toenail. But as he turned
to leave, Fred opened his eyes. "Hey, who
goes there?"

Joe dashed down the hall, climbed
out the bathroom window, and dropped
into the backyard. Suddenly lights came
on all over the grounds.

Joe looked for a place to hide. He jumped into the Jacuzzi just as Fred came running out the back door. Joe stayed low, out of sight.

After a while Fred went back inside and turned off the lights.

Joe still held the piece of toenail he needed to clone Fred. When the coast was clear, he climbed out of the warm water and headed for his lair.

"Should have rented the one with the Jacuzzi," he said to himself. It would be a great way to wind down after a long day of devious and sinister deeds.

MEANWHILE . . .

While Joe the Bad Guy was getting ready to clone a Fred, Melvin and Candace were at Big Al's Rent-a-Lair, trapped inside a lair with a Jacuzzi. Outside, the big Rottweiler crashed against the door, snapping his teeth and growling.

Melvin had to find a way out. He knew it was up to him alone. Candace was too busy staring at the Jacuzzi and dreaming of getting her own lair to be of any help in the thinking department.

"What if I don't call it a lair?" she said. "What if I just call it a fort, or a clubhouse?"

"We need to find a way out of here," Melvin said as he watched Candace checking the water temperature.

"Want to take a dip, Melvin?"

Melvin looked out the window at the snarling dog. "No time for swimming, Candace. We have to get out of here before the sun comes up. If Big Al catches us, we'll go to jail. Do you know what they do to superheroes who go to jail?"

Candace shook her head.

"They take their capes away."

Candace stopped playing with the water. She looked around. Then she spotted something on the ceiling and pointed. "What's that?"

"Holy escape route! It's a hatch to let the steam out."

Holy escape route, indeed! It was a way out for Candace, but how about for Melvin, Mr. Crash–Splat–Thud–Kabonk? Candace could get off the ground in one try. Melvin could not, and he needed more running room to launch himself.

Candace flew up to the ceiling and opened the hatch. "Come on, Melvin."

Melvin shook his head, knowing it was hopeless even to try. But wait a minute, he thought. He was a superhero. And he was as fast as a speeding bullet. He could outrun a dog.

"Candace, can you distract the dog?"

"I can imitate a hamburger like you wouldn't believe."

"Perfect," Melvin said. "Go for it and I'll meet you on the street."

Candace flew to the far side of the lot and did the best impression of a hamburger the world has ever known.

The dog moved away from the door, and Melvin ran for it. It was no contest. He was as fast as a speeding bullet, all

right. Maybe faster. Once outside Big Al's, he launched himself.

Crash!

Splat!

Thud!

Kabonk!

He was up and flying in five, then he saw Candace home safely. It wasn't part of the Superhero's Code to do this. Melvin just liked looking after his partner in uncrime. Tomorrow they'd do some math, then start going down their list of bad guys. The Grateful Fred had to be protected.

"See you tomorrow, Candace," Melvin said as he flew off.

"Squeakity squeak?" said Hugo the rat when Melvin arrived back at the tree

house. Hugo was either trying to explain the last episode of *The Adventures of Thunderman* or he wanted to play a game of Monopoly. Melvin wasn't sure. But right now he had other things to think about. He pulled out his list of bad guys and read it again. Where to begin? he thought.

He'd start at the top—who was Max the Wonder Thug anyway?

THREE FREDS ARE BETTER THAN ONE

Back at his lair, Joe the Bad Guy decided to clone three Freds for starters. He could always add more later. He placed Fred's toenail on the ground and zapped it with the Clone-o-Matic 6000. This was what he meant to do, at least. But his aim was off. Instead of zapping the toenail, he zapped a cockroach. Now there were two. He tried again—ZAAAAAAP! Another miss. Now he had two sets of dirty dishes. Again he tried, but he only succeeded in duplicating the cobwebs hanging off the couch.

Concentrate, he told himself. His lair was getting worse and worse.

Only he couldn't concentrate. He was too excited about finally getting his revenge. His aim was all over the place. Here a ZAP, there a ZAP, everywhere a ZAP, ZAP. Two half-eaten pizzas. Two copies of *Bad Guy's Digest*. Two piles of dirty underwear.

Finally, he got it right. He zapped Fred's toenail dead center—ZAAAAAAP! A cloud of dust erupted and spun around like a tornado. It rose to the height of a full-grown man. When everything settled, there stood a Fred, fully clothed, the spitting image of the original.

"He's the spitting image of the original," Joe said.

He made two more Freds and stood back to admire his work.

"Master," the Freds said, "your wish is our command."

Joe decided to send Fred One to rob a bank, Fred Two to steal a car, and Fred Three to cause general trouble. "And make sure people see you," he told them. "If possible, get yourself on tape."

Joe didn't want there to be any doubt that it was Fred of The Grateful Fred doing all these dastardly deeds . . . or sinister deeds, for that matter.

The Freds turned to leave.

"Wait a minute," Joe said as an idea popped into his head. He'd send the Freds out in due time, but first things first. "Fred One, make me a tuna sandwich, extra pickle. Fred Two, grab the broom and sweep up this lair.

And get those cockroaches, while you're at it. Fred Three, massage my feet." As long as his wish was their command, Joe was going to take advantage.

He didn't send off the Freds until he'd eaten three triple-decker sandwiches. And now his lair absolutely sparkled. His walls were still dented, of course, but they were the cleanest dents he'd ever seen.

The Freds left. Joe's plan was going perfectly. And his feet felt great! There was only one thing that could mess it up. And that was Melvin Beederman.

But Joe had supplies on hand in case anything went wrong in the Melvin department. Fortunately, he knew about Melvin's major weakness. Everyone did, since it had once been blabbed to the world on the Unofficial Melvin Beeder-man Web site. The Web site no longer existed, but the damage had been done. Everyone knew what made Melvin lose his strength, including Joe the Bad Guy.

It was bologna, the gourmet lunch meat itself. Bologna was to Melvin what kryptonite was to Superman. And Joe had stocked up on it, just in case.

If Melvin came near, Joe would be ready for him.

"Melvin Beederman doesn't have a chance," Joe said to himself. "Neither does Fred."

THAT'S USING YOUR FREDS

The Freds went to work. Fred One robbed the First National Bank on Sunset, pausing and looking up at the cameras so there would be no doubt about who to arrest for the crime. Then he ran. For the plan to work, none of the Freds could be caught.

Fred Two spent most of the day looking for just the right car to steal. He knew that the more expensive the car, the more trouble the real Fred would be in. You had to be choosy in this situation. And Fred Two was. He hot-wired a Ferrari and raced through the city, then headed back to Joe the Bad Guy's lair.

Fred Three had been asked to cause general trouble. This gave him a ton of options. Should he steal something? Break something? Beat up someone? The possibilities were endless. He decided he'd start with bullying and work his way up to more serious crimes.

He went to the nearest school and waited for the bell to ring. As the students headed home for the day, Fred chose the smallest one to pick on.

"Hey, you," Fred Three said, closing in on a second-grader. "Hey, twerp."

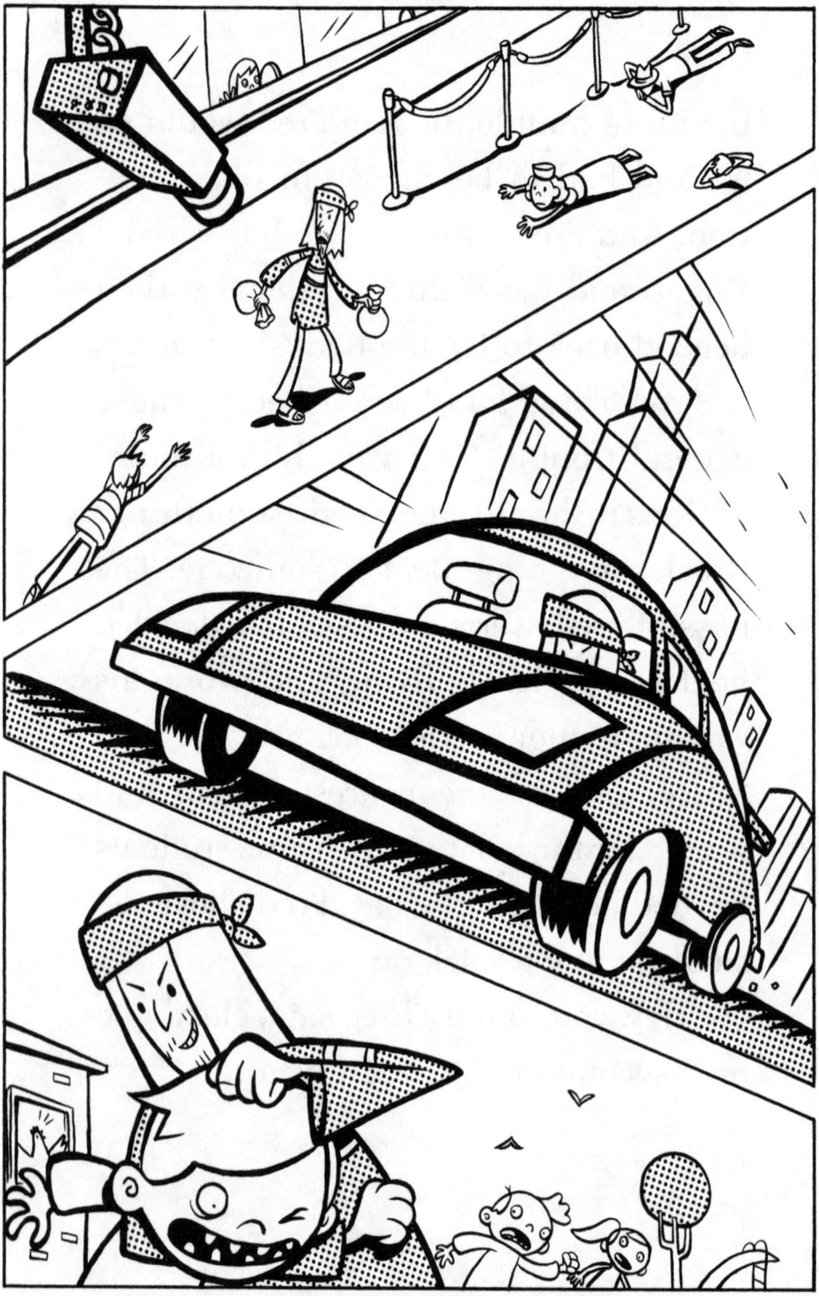

The second-grader stopped and looked at Fred. He'd been told never to speak to strangers, but here was someone who knew his name. How did this man know his name was Twerp? Timothy Twerp Junior the Third, if you wanted the long version.

"Do I know you?" Timothy asked Fred. The fact was, he thought he recognized Fred from someplace. Maybe on the cover of one of his mother's CDs.

"You look hungry, kid," Fred said.

It was one thing to talk to a stranger, but to take food from one was a definite no-no. Timothy turned and began to walk away. "I'm not hungry," he called over his shoulder. "Thanks anyway, mister."

"Seriously, kid. You look hungry. How about a knuckle sandwich?"

Knuckle sandwich! The worst food Timothy could imagine. His walk turned into a run, then into a sprint—pretty darn fast, too, for a second-grader.

But he was no match for Fred, who caught up with the kid in no time and delivered a couple of choice knuckle sandwiches right in front of the automated teller machine on Wilshire, where his every move was captured on video. Fred looked up and said, "Cheeeeeeese." He was glad that he'd brushed his teeth earlier that day. He wanted to look good for the evening news.

Back at his lair, Joe the Bad Guy was getting anxious. He couldn't wait to see if the three Freds accomplished their missions. He cloned ten more Freds while he was waiting and sent them off.

"Rob, steal, and break stuff," he told them. "Make sure someone sees you, and don't get caught. Meet back here this evening." He would have had them stay to clean up the lair first, but Freds One, Two, and Three had done a pretty good job.

The Freds took off and Joe watched them from the door of his lair. "I feel like a father," he said.

It didn't take long for the news to get out. Los Angeles was in the midst of a crime spree, the likes of which hadn't

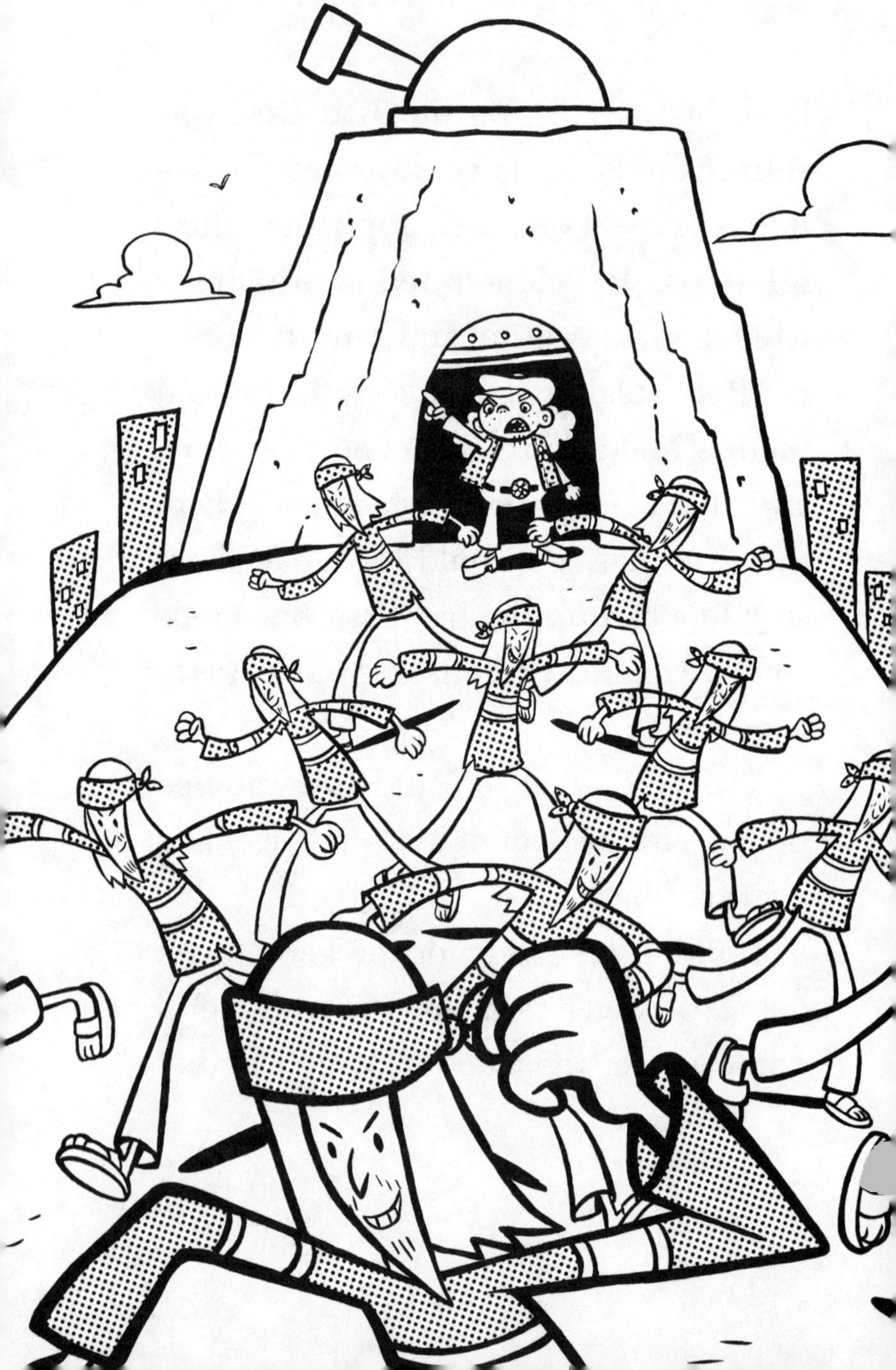

been seen since Max the Wonder Thug's second cousin had robbed fourteen banks in a single day . . . or was it Calamity Wayne's third niece? In any case, bad stuff was happening. And all fingers pointed to one man—Fred of The Grateful Fred.

UNLUCKY THIRTEEN

There were thirteen Freds out and about, doing dastardly deeds. And, as everyone knows, thirteen is an unlucky number.

It sure was unlucky for young Winston Clarkwood. He had been minding his own business, walking home from school, when a red Ferrari jumped the curb and came roaring down the sidewalk toward him.

Winston dived into the street just in time. Just in the nick of time, to be exact. He tore his pants and skinned his knee, not to mention his face.

He got to his feet, took a deep breath, and continued on his way. A few minutes later he passed the First National Bank just as a man burst from the front door, holding a bag of money. He ran right over Winston. There was no getting out of the way this time. More skinned knees. Another face-plant into the concrete.

Winston got up slowly and stumbled on. Funny, he thought, the bank robber looked just like the man in the red car. Exactly like him in fact. How could that be?

It was a confusing and painful day for young Winston Clarkwood. He'd had painful days before, and he'd had confusing ones. But this was the first time he had both on the same day. And the problem was, his day wasn't over yet.

He moved on, keeping an eye peeled for the guy in the red sports car, or his bank robbing twin. His face was tired of meeting the ground up close and personal.

Suddenly Winston saw him. The sports car man, the bank robber dude. "Don't tell me there are three of them," he said.

"Actually, there are thirteen of us," the man told him, blocking his path. "The name's Fred. Stick 'em up."

Winston blinked. *This can't be happening,* he thought. *Somebody wake me when it's over.*

"Your money or your life."

Winston just stood there, not believing his own ears.

When he didn't move, Fred turned him upside down until every last coin fell out of his pockets. Then he grabbed the money and walked off. "Pleasure doing business with you, kid."

It wasn't very pleasant for Winston Clarkwood. But at least he didn't hit the ground for a third time that day.

When Fred left, Winston ran the rest of the way home. Los Angeles was no place for a kid on his own, he decided.

That evening he was quiet

at dinner. He did his homework in his room and fell asleep early. This was one day he wanted to forget.

But when Winston closed his eyes he saw the same face—Fred's face. He had one nightmare after another. He woke up screaming.

His mother came running. "What is it, Winston?"

He was shivering under his covers. He didn't say a word.

"Winston?" his mother asked. "What's wrong?"

He sat up and poked his head out from under his blankets. "Mom?"

"Yes?"

"I—I—"

"For goodness' sakes, what is it?"

He swallowed hard. "I see Fred people."

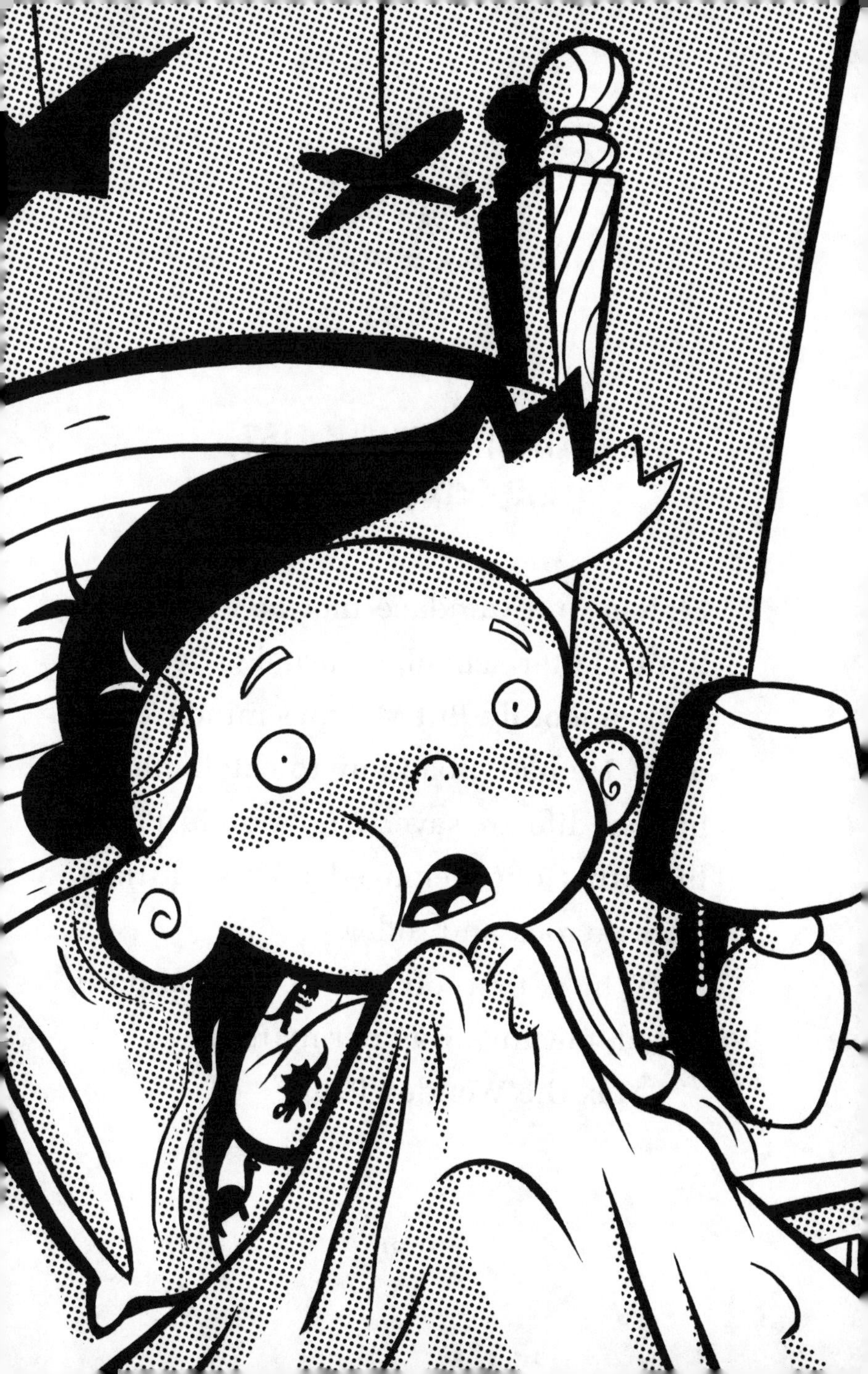

TAKING THEIR LIST, CHECKING IT TWICE

Melvin and Candace met at the public library after school, as usual. The math went smoothly. But Melvin's mind wasn't on it. He had a bad guy to catch, plus a human life to save. And not just any life—this one belonged to his all-time favorite rock and roller.

"Who's first on the list?" Candace asked, putting away her math book.

"Max the Wonder Thug."

They went to the address listed on the sales receipt and knocked on the door. Max opened it. His neck was almost as wide as his shoulders. Melvin asked Max where he was the night of the concert.

"Let me see," Max said, scratching his oversized neck. "Oh yeah, I was robbing the bank on Fifth and Wilshire."

"You were nowhere near The Grateful Fred concert?"

"Nope. Just robbing a bank."

"Well, that's okay then," Melvin said, "as long as you were just robbing a bank. Thank you for your time."

Max closed the door, and Melvin and Candace moved on.

"Next?" Candace asked.

Melvin checked the list. "Stinky Gillespie." He made a face. "Not another smelly bad guy."

Smelly bad guys were Melvin's least favorite type of bad guy. He didn't know if there were any sweet-smelling bad guys, but he could always hope.

They went to Stinky's lair and knocked on the door. The smell greeted them first.

When the door opened it grew worse—much worse. Melvin and Candace pinched their noses.

"Are you Stinky Gillespie?" Melvin asked in a high voice.

"In the flesh. If you're collecting for the Bad-Guy Retirement Fund, I've already donated."

"We aren't collecting anything," Melvin assured him. "Just one quick question."

"A real quick question," Candace blurted as her eyes began to water.

"Where were you on the night of the Grateful Fred Concert?"

Stinky paused to think about it. "Let's see. Was I on a jewelry heist that night? No, that's not it. Liquor store robbery?

No, that was Monday night. Oh, right, I believe I was stealing TVs that night. Hey, that reminds me. Can I make either of you a deal on a thirty-two-inch Zenith?"

"No, that's okay," Melvin answered. He and Candace turned to leave.

"If you know anyone, send them my way," Stinky said. "The TVs may be hot, but the price is right. I also sell jewelry and . . . uh . . . pretty much anything I can get my hands on."

"Thanks anyway," Melvin said.

"Yeah, thanks." Candace tugged on Melvin's cape to get them downwind as soon as possible. "I'm glad he wasn't the one we're looking for," she said.

Melvin looked at her and nodded. "I know what you mean. How do you capture a bad guy while holding your nose at the same time?"

"Exactly. So who's next on the list?"

"Calamity Wayne."

And so it went—all day long. Calamity Wayne, the McNasty Sisters— every bad guy they talked to had been committing other crimes the night of the concert.

But there were still more names on the list. Was one of them out to get The Grateful Fred?

ARREST THAT FRED!

Thirteen Freds were committing crimes. And that's a lot of Freds, no matter who's counting. Robbing banks, swiping cars, stealing lunch money—these guys didn't mess around.

But the real Fred didn't know any of this. He didn't watch much TV and hadn't been reading the papers. He'd been too busy fixing his guitars. Someone had broken into his house and cut all the strings, the same person who'd given him a midnight toenail trim. There's nothing worse than having your toenails trimmed by a criminal.

Fred went about fixing his guitars the way he went about everything in life—with a song in his head. And to him, everything was a song. The sky is blue, yeah, yeah, baby. What's for breakfast? Yeah, yeah, baby. Melvin can see my underwear! Yeah, yeah, baby. This was just the way it was. The Rock and Roller's Code was in his blood. Songs were everywhere.

And so, despite having to fix seventeen guitars all at once, it was a pretty good day for Fred.

Or at least it was until the police showed up.

Someone's at my door. Yeah, yeah, baby.

"What can I do for you, officers?" Fred said out loud when he opened the front door, and in his head, *Yeah, yeah, baby.*

"You're under arrest," the police told him.

"Arrest? What for?" Fred couldn't believe his ears. He also couldn't believe the policemen's mouths. There went his happy day—*poof!*

"You name it. Bank robbery, grand theft, stealing pocket change from schoolchildren."

"You have the wrong guy," Fred said as they dragged him away. "I'm telling you, this is a big mistake!"

"Save your breath, Fred. We have eye-witnesses, and we have you on tape. You're going to jail for a very long time."

"I want to talk to my lawyer," Fred yelled. He thought this over. "No, wait. Get me Melvin Beederman!"

Later that day, the police threw Fred into a jail cell with a stinky criminal named Stan. Fred made the bad mistake of breathing through his nose. *Holy burning nostrils!* he thought. This had to be the second stinkiest bad guy in Los Angeles.

Holy burning nostrils, indeed! He *was* the second stinkiest guy in Los Angeles.

"What ya in fer?" Stan asked.

Fred pinched his nose and spoke in a high voice. "They have the wrong guy."

"That's what they all say on the first day. You'll come clean with me, sooner or later. And I can keep yer secret, don't you worry." He walked over and shook

Fred's hand. "My name's Gillespie. You may have heard of my brother, Stinky Gillespie."

Just what I need, Fred thought, *Stinky's kid brother as a roommate.*

It was going to be a long and smelly night for Fred. He stood at the bars of his cell, trying to get air and singing, "Nobody knows the trouble I've seen. Yeah, yeah, baby."

No one believed Fred was innocent. Somehow he had to get a message to Melvin Beederman. Melvin would believe him—and he'd know what to do.

THIRTEEN FREDS,
THIRTEEN PAIRS OF UNDERWEAR

The TV was on when Melvin arrived back at his tree house. *The Adventures of Thunderman* was long over, and Hugo the rat was now watching the local news.

Melvin could hardly believe his eye-balls. There on the TV screen he saw Fred of The Grateful Fred, handcuffed and yelling to the reporters, "You can't do this to me! I'm innocent. Melvin Beederman, help me!"

A moment later Melvin's phone rang. It was Fred. They'd given him one phone call and this was it.

Melvin listened to Fred and watched the TV at the same time. In his ear he heard that Fred was innocent, but what he saw with his own eyes was a whole other story. The bank robbery was caught on tape. So was the car theft. The reporter said that even the fingerprints matched. It was an open-and-shut case. Fred was going to prison for a long time.

But in his ear Fred was pleading his case. "I can't explain what you're seeing on the TV," Fred said, "but that is not me. Something funky is going on. Melvin, I need your help."

It was hard to say no to his favorite rock and roller. Just talking to Fred made "Yeah, Yeah, Baby" pop into Melvin's head.

"Can you help me, Melvin?" Fred asked. "Will you?"

"Yeah, baby."

"Pardon?"

"I mean, yes, I'll get to the bottom of this." Melvin hung up. There were still a few more names on the list to go through. He and Candace would get cracking first thing after math.

The next day, they raced through Candace's math homework. Melvin was in a hurry to clear Fred's good name. Candace was not so sure.

"It looked an awful lot like him on TV, Melvin. Fingerprints and everything."

"Call it a hunch," Melvin said. "Something funky is going on."

"A hunch? Is that anything like noggin power?"

"Kind of." Melvin took out his list and looked at it. "Goofball McClusky. Maybe we'll get lucky."

They went to the address on the receipt. It was an enormous double-decker lair. Candace couldn't help herself.

She started drooling. Melvin knocked on the door.

Goofball McClusky opened it. Behind him, they saw steam rising.

"Look," Candace whispered, "a double-decker lair with a Jacuzzi! All I have is a lousy bedroom."

"Shhh," Melvin said and turned to Goofball. "Mr. McClusky, where were you on the night of The Grateful Fred concert?"

"I was working, of course. Robbed a few jewelry stores on Rodeo Drive."

"Oh, you were just robbing jewelry stores."

"Yes, it was a good night. I'm thinking of upgrading to a triple-decker lair."

"Triple decker!" Candace said with wide eyes.

"Thank you for your time, Mr. McClusky," Melvin said. He turned to leave, pulling Candace with him.

"Did you hear that, Melvin? A triple-decker lair!"

"Focus, Candace," Melvin told her. "We have work to do." He pulled out his list of names and looked at it. "Only one more left, Joe the Bad Guy. Let's hope this last one is our man."

They went to Joe the Bad Guy's lair and knocked on the door. Joe answered.

"Hello, I'm Melvin—"

"Melvin Beederman. Come in, come in," Joe said with a smirk. "Can I offer you a root beer?"

Melvin's ears perked. Root beer was his favorite. Candace's too. "I'd love a root beer."

"Help yourselves," Joe said.

Melvin and Candace went to the fridge, opened the door, and— BOLOGNA! It was their only weakness. And the whole fridge was packed with it.

The partners in uncrime fell to their knees.

"Can't . . . move . . . get . . . me . . . out . . . of . . . here."

Joe laughed. "I was hoping you'd show up, Melvin Beederman."

Melvin looked at Candace. "I can't believe I fell for it," he gasped. "The old bologna-in-the-refrigerator trick."

Joe the Bad Guy grabbed some rope and tied their hands behind their backs. Then he bound their feet, his smirk getting bigger by the second. Melvin and Candace knew it would do no good to resist, not with the bologna right there in front of them.

"Looks like Fred will be in jail for many years to come, thanks to the Clone-o-Matic 6000," Joe said with a kind of mean laugh (he still hadn't read the book on evil ones). "Well, I'm off to dispose of the extra Freds."

He went to a door in the back of the lair and opened it. "Guys," he called, "let's go. And turn off the TV." He turned to Melvin and Candace. "They love watching *The Adventures of Thunderman*."

Joe stepped back and suddenly the room was filled with Freds, each one the spitting image of the original. Thirteen Freds, thirteen pairs of underwear. Poor Melvin!

"Roll call," Joe said. "Fred?"

"Here."

"Fred?"

"Here."

He went through all thirteen of them. To Melvin and Candace he said, "Once these Freds are history there will be no evidence. The real Fred will be blamed. And I will be long gone."

The Freds went outside and loaded themselves into a van.

Joe stayed inside and struck a match. "Looks like I won't be needing this lair anymore." He tossed the burning match into a wastebasket and kicked it over, spreading flames across the floor. "Adios, amigos," he said, then he ran for the van and took off.

Candace turned to Melvin as the flames spread to the furniture and drapes. "What do we do now?"

"Don't look at me," he said. "I'm not the narrator."

JOE THE BRAINLESS

The door to the fridge was open and our two superheroes were tied up close by. Flames rose to the ceiling. Smoke was everywhere.

"Seriously, Melvin, what's your noggin telling us to do?" Candace asked.

"I have no idea." Melvin couldn't believe his bad luck. It seemed the whole world knew of his weakness. And here he was, once again, powerless before bologna.

The room grew hotter. They could hardly breathe.

"Come on," Candace said, coughing. "If anyone can think of a plan, you can."

True, Melvin was the one with noggin power. He and Candace had been in worse scrapes than this and he'd always gotten them out.

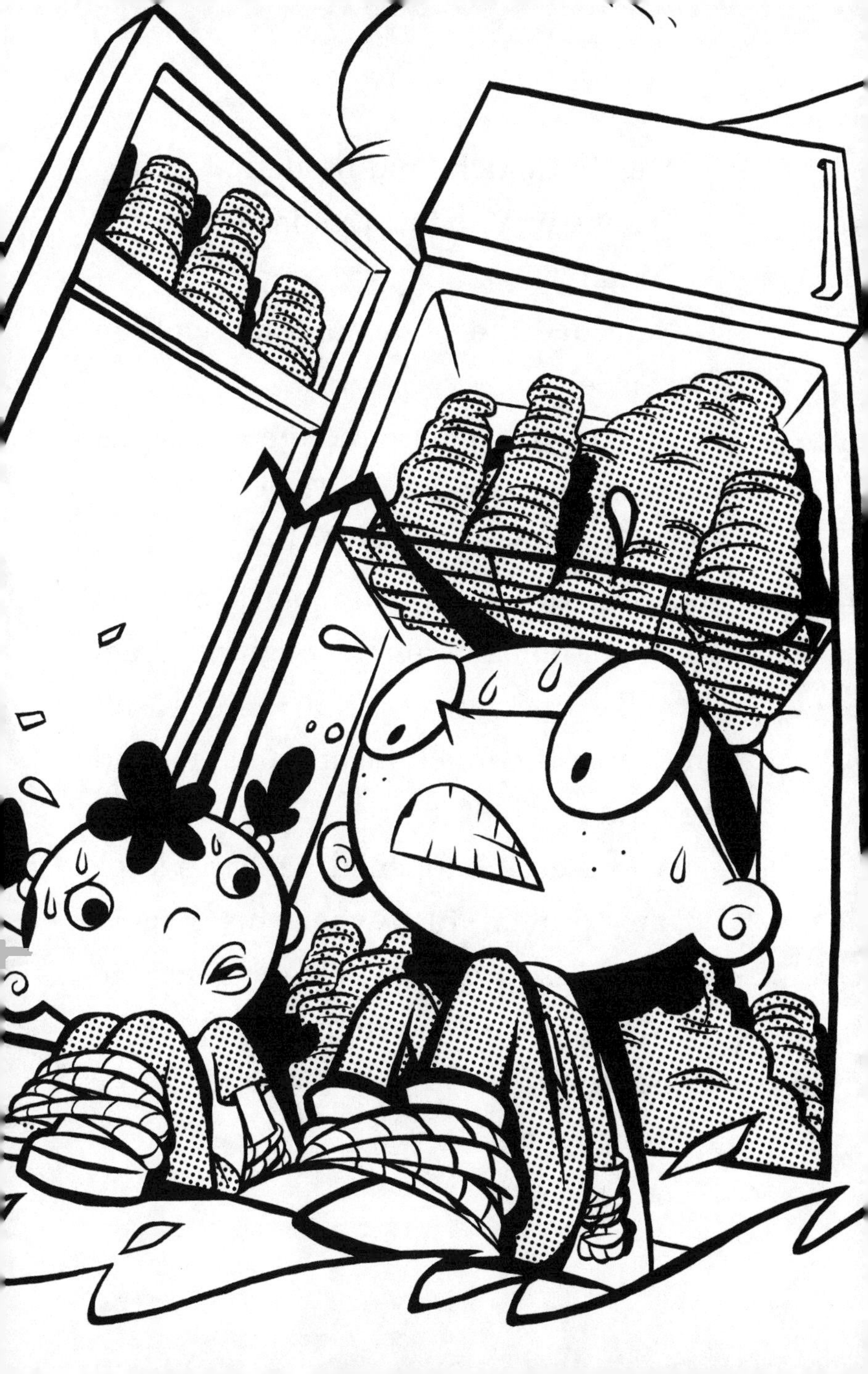

Melvin thought and thought.

"That's it, Melvin," Candace said.

"What?"

"You had that 'I'm thinking' look on your face."

Melvin glanced around the room. The flames were spreading. There was still time—but not a lot. If only he could find some sandwich wrap to block out the effects of bologna long enough for them to make their escape. But there wasn't any—just the lunch meat he hated, and way too much of it.

And then it happened. Melvin's knee began to itch. Just when his noggin power was kicking in. As everyone knows, you can't be itchy and think at the same time.

Melvin began to sweat. He made a face.

"What is it?" Candace asked. He no longer had that 'I'm thinking' look.

"I have an itch."

"Maybe I can reach it." Candace stretched her fingers toward him—and the ropes snapped. "What the—" She moved her legs and snapped those ropes, too. "Hey, Melvin, I'm free! Let's get out of here."

"How'd you do that?"

"I don't know. Try to break the ropes. I don't think we've lost our superhero powers after all."

Melvin snapped the ropes binding his hands and ankles. He and Candace stood up, flames roaring around them.

Melvin pointed to the open door of the fridge. "That wasn't Joe the Bad Guy. It was Joe the Brainless. Look, it's not bologna. It's pastrami! Let's get out of here."

They did. Just in time. Just in the nick of time, in fact. The house began to collapse around them, and Candace kicked down the front door to make a way out. She might have been able to open the door using the knob like normal people do. But kicking down doors was a Candace thing.

Once outside, Melvin looked for any sign of Joe the Bad Guy's van. "We have to find him before he does away with the Freds. Up, up, and away."

Crash!

Splat!

Thud!

Kabonk!

Up and flying in five as usual. The two of them flew off to rescue the Freds. Problem was, where to look?

They zoomed between the tall buildings of downtown Los Angeles. Melvin saw his reflection all over the place, but didn't stop to flex. There was no time. He had to save all the other Freds to save the real one. If not, his favorite rock and roller was doomed to many years behind bars.

The partners searched and searched. Downtown. Up in the hills. Throughout the valley. Out to the beach.

"I see something," Candace called. Sure enough, it was Joe the Bad Guy's van. It had left the road and was shooting across a grassy knoll toward the edge of a cliff overlooking the Pacific Ocean. Melvin and Candace raced to the rescue.

They dropped before the van, stopping it cold. "Come out of there with your hands up," yelled Candace.

Melvin elbowed her and whispered something in her ear.

"I mean—not so fast!" She looked at her partner in uncrime. "Better?"

"Much," Melvin said.

Joe the Bad Guy stepped from the van, leaving the Freds inside. "I should have known that I couldn't outwit the famous Melvin Beederman and his lovely assistant."

Candace smiled. No one had ever called her lovely before.

"You two are just too good," Joe went on. "You fly, you stop speeding vans. I bet you're even faster than a speeding bullet."

Melvin stuck out his chest. "We are."

"Yes, like I said, you two are too smart

and too powerful. Do you mind if I squeeze your bicep?"

Melvin flexed. He'd been wanting to all day.

Joe gave Melvin's bicep a squeeze. "Awesome. Like iron. And how sharp you look in your superhero outfits. What is that, silk?"

Candace and Melvin exchanged a look. Maybe Joe was bad heading toward dreadful, but right now he was laying on the charm and laying it on thick. "I wish I had a camera. It's not every day that a bad guy gets to—"

"Melvin, the van!" Candace yelled.

Melvin turned. The van was heading toward the cliff. It had no driver—and all thirteen Freds were inside. There was no time to launch himself. He ran while Candace flew, fast as a speeding bullet. Maybe faster. They heard Joe laughing as they raced to catch up.

"Too late. The Freds are history."

Not if Melvin Beederman had anything to say about it! He ran so fast the grass burned beneath his feet. Candace streaked through the air above him.

The van went over the cliff and plunged toward the jagged rocks below. So did the partners in uncrime. Melvin ran straight down the side of the cliff and whipped around the front of the van.

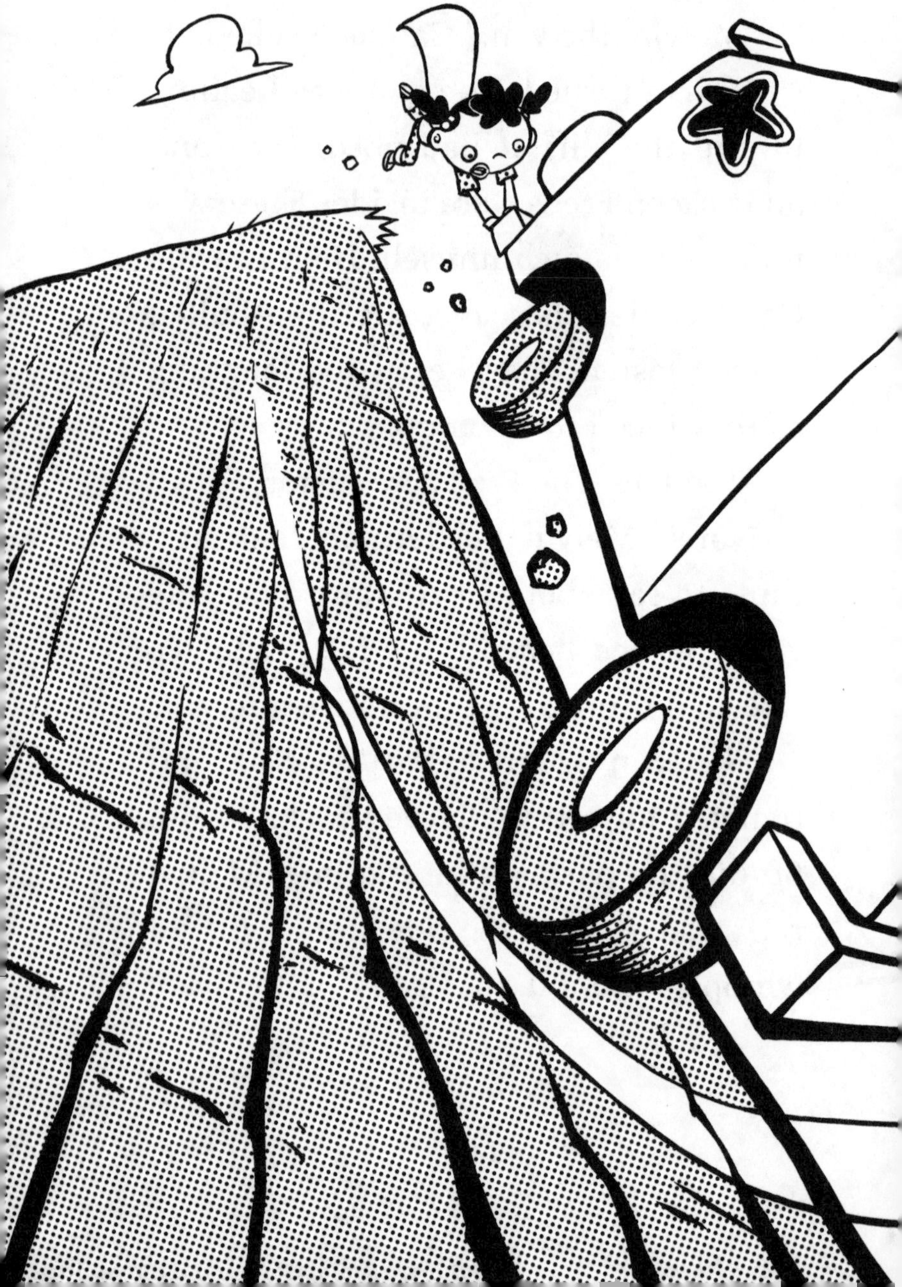

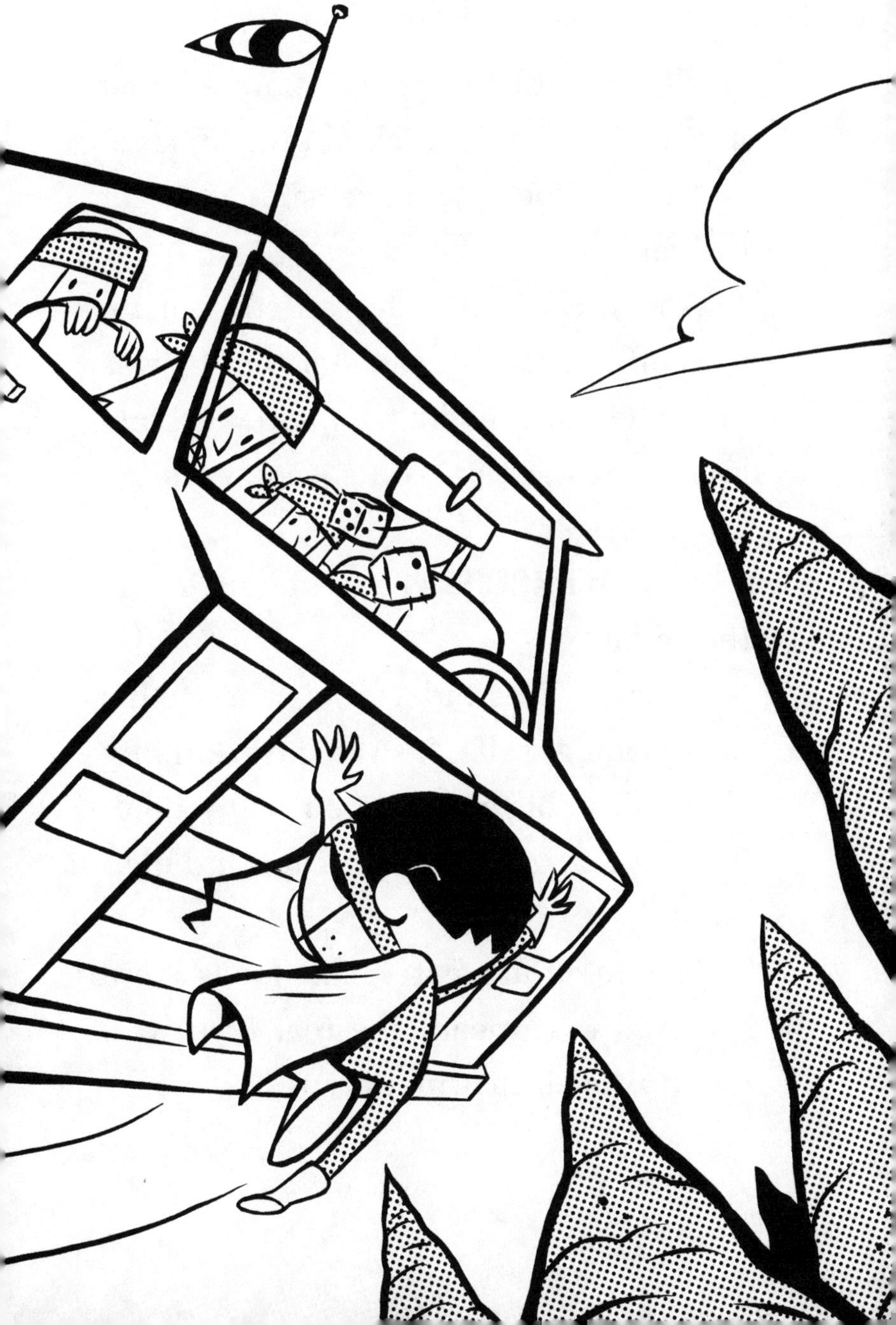

Candace grabbed the rear bumper, just in time. Just in the nick of time, in fact.

"Go get Joe," Candace said. "I've got the van."

And Melvin did. He ran straight up the cliff. Joe had a head start but he was no match for Melvin, who, as everybody knows, was as fast as a speeding bullet. Maybe faster.

"Not so fast!" he said, grabbing Joe by the collar.

"Curses," Joe said. He was back to his uncharming self. "I was just kidding about your bicep. And you really don't look all that great in your cape and high boots."

Melvin didn't care. The Freds were safe and that meant the real Fred was, too. It was all that mattered.

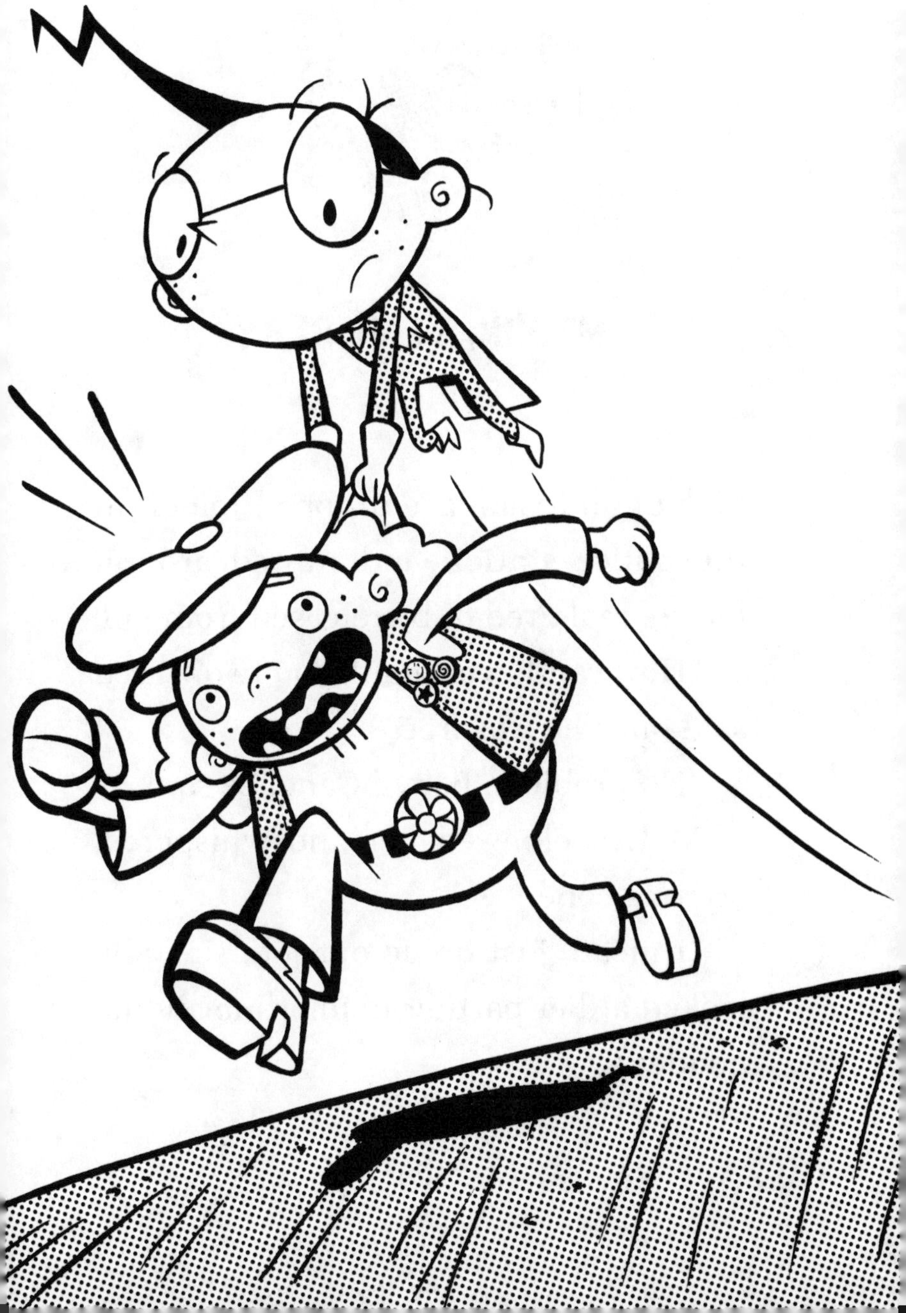

MELVIN, YEAH, BABY

Melvin and Candace dropped Joe off at the police station and waited around for the real Fred to be released from jail.

"How can I ever thank you two?" Fred said once he was free.

"No problem, baby," Candace said.

Melvin elbowed her and whispered, "Wrong code."

"I mean, just doing our job, sir." She looked at her partner in uncrime and he nodded.

She was finally learning the superhero lingo.

"Well, thanks again," Fred said. "I'm
grateful."

"Yes," Melvin said. "You are The Grateful Fred."

Melvin saw Candace safely home, then returned to his tree house. His pet rat Hugo was there waiting for him.

"Squeaker squeakity?" Hugo said.

"Squeaker squeakity is right," Melvin replied. He had no idea what he had said, but at the moment he didn't care. He was just glad his favorite rock-and-roll band was still able to play music, thanks to him and Candace.

A few weeks later, The Grateful Fred put out a new song. "Melvin, Yeah, Baby" went straight to the top of the charts.

Fred had written it in honor of his favorite superheroes. He named it after

Melvin but it was about both of them—the partners in uncrime. And Melvin Beederman listened to it again and again. Standing in his tree house, looking out over the city of Los Angeles, he was glad to be a superhero. He didn't know when his next adventure would come . . . but he knew he and Candace would be ready.

As for the Freds, it was soon discovered that the Clone-o-Matic had a goodness and niceness switch as well as a devious and sinister one. It was simply a matter of using the proper switch setting and re-zapping them. All over town the Freds were doing good deeds. They helped old ladies cross the street, picked up trash along the highway, and helped first-graders learn to read.

Yep, things were looking pretty good in Los Angeles. At least for the time being. And the city had Melvin Beederman and Candace Brinkwater to thank for it.

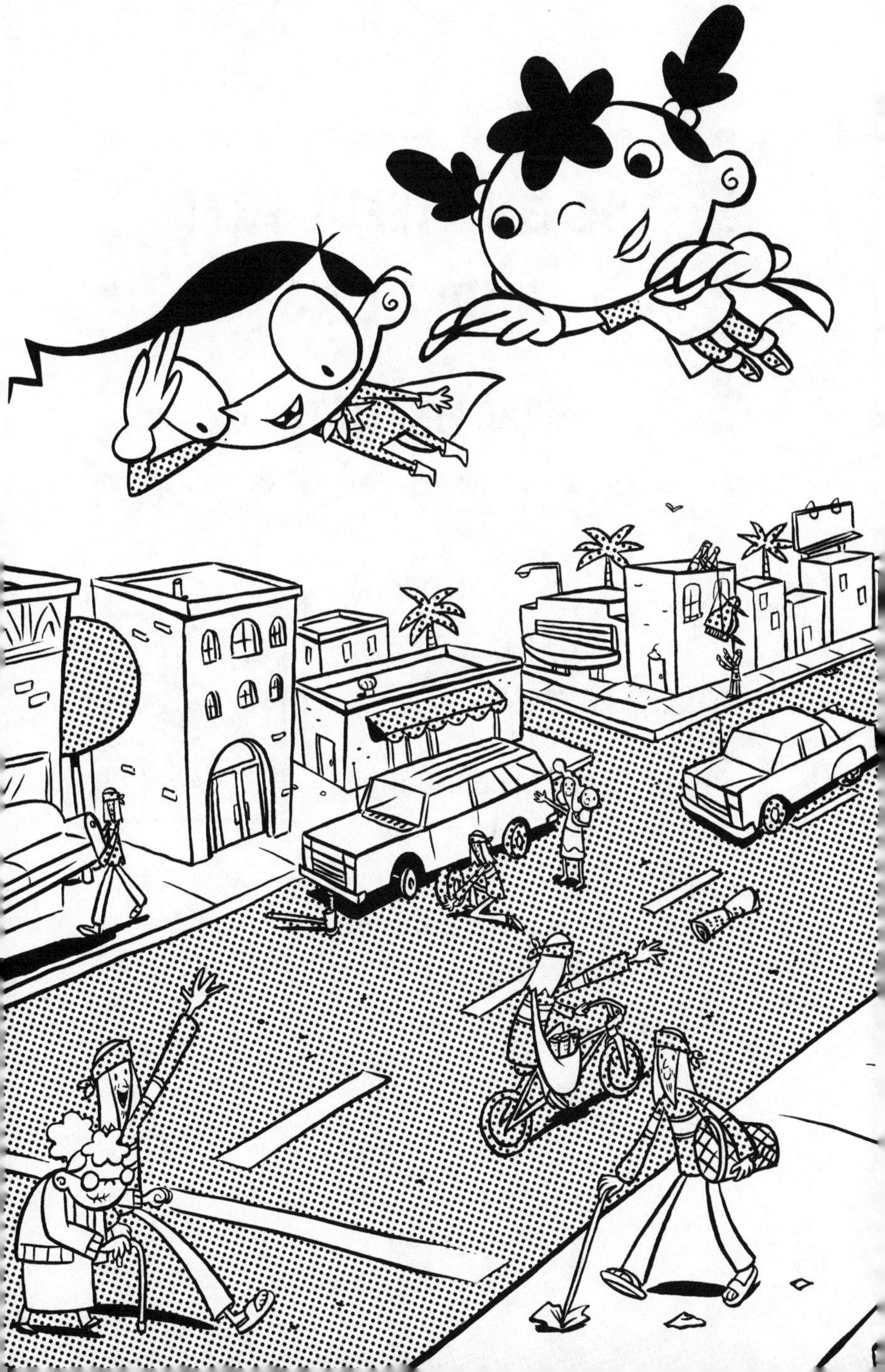

THE GRATEFUL FRED AUDITIONS

★ THE FINALISTS ★

TONE-DEAF TESSY

★ Sang "Yeah, Yeah, Baby" in the key of H (a very difficult task, since there is no key of H)
★ The judges were unanimous: "Oh, my aching eardrums!"

HOLD-YOUR-EARS BILLY

* His name says it all
* The judges were too
  busy holding their ears to listen
* Billy now pumps gas in Duluth

ONE-HUNDRED-DECIBEL DAVE

* This guy doesn't need
  a microphone
* Blew the toupee off one of the
  male judges
* Gave a female judge a new hairdo—
  at no extra charge!

MELVIN, YEAH, BABY
LYRICS BY THE GRATEFUL FRED
(to the tune of "She Loves You" by the Beatles)

Melvin, yeah, yeah, yeah.
Melvin, yeah, yeah, yeah.
Melvin, yeah, yeah, yeah, yeah—
Baby.

Well, Melvin came to town,
And bad guys best beware–ee–air
When he gets off the ground
He can see your underwear–ee–air.

'Cause he is Melvin
And you know he runs so fast.
'Cause he is Melvin
And he never comes in last.
Ooo!

Melvin, yeah, yeah, yeah.
Melvin, yeah, yeah, yeah.
Melvin, yeah, yeah, yeah, yeah—
Baby.

Melvin and Candace, too,
They are partners in uncrime–ee-ime.
Though bad guys smell like poo,
They stop them all the time–ee-ime.

'Cause he is Melvin
And you know he runs so fast.
'Cause he is Melvin
And he never comes in last.
Ooo!

Melvin, yeah, yeah, yeah.
Melvin, yeah, yeah, yeah.
Melvin, yeah, yeah, yeah, yeah—
Baby.

And now, a superheroic excerpt from

DOOM WITH A VIEW

Superhero Melvin Beederman was minding his own business, doing what he did second-best. What he did best, of course, was save the world, chase down bad guys, make the city of Los Angeles a better place to live. But he wasn't doing that. He was doing his second-best activity—hanging out in his tree house hideout, eating pretzels with his pet rat Hugo, and watching his favorite TV

show—*The Adventures of Thunderman.*
Thunderman and his assistant Thunder
Thighs also saved the world. In every
single episode. Watching them always
inspired Melvin to do his job a little
better.

When the show was over, Melvin
decided to check his e-mail before
starting his day.

"I think I'll go save the world," he said
to Hugo, his pet rat.

"*Squeak,*" Hugo said in reply.

This either meant "You do that, kind
sir." Or maybe it was "Are
you sure you don't want to
have a push-up contest?"

Melvin was never
sure what Hugo
was saying.

Though he had once been fluent in gerbil, talking to a rat was another story. He turned on his computer and found only one e-mail waiting for him. But it was a doozy.

I'm coming to get you, Melvin Beederman. Don't try to hide. I know all your tricks and your weaknesses. And when I find you, you'll be toast! Smashed-beneath-my-feet toast.
Your loving enemy,
SC
P.S. Consider yourself doomed!

SC? Melvin didn't know any SC. He caught bad guys for a living, it was true. So there were plenty of people who wanted revenge. But who was SC? Melvin thought about some of his recent battles. Joe the Bad Guy? No, wrong initials. The McNasty Brothers? No, couldn't be.

Melvin looked at the return address of the e-mail for a clue: imgoingtogetyou@ ifitsthelastthingido.badguy. "Holy mystery!" Melvin said out loud.

"This ain't good."

Holy mystery, indeed! It wasn't (narrators never say "ain't").

There was only one thing to do, Melvin decided. He had to talk it over with his partner in uncrime, Candace Brinkwater. He always felt better talking to Candace. Unlike Melvin, who was an orphan and had graduated from the

Superhero's Academy, Candace lived in a normal house with her family. She was not from the academy. She was just a girl with whom Melvin had divided his cape. As they say, two superheroes are better than one. And Los Angeles was happy to have both of them.

"See you later, Hugo," Melvin said as he moved to the door of the tree house.

"*Squeak*," Hugo replied, which either meant "Go get 'em, tiger" or "How do you spell kumquat?"

Melvin wasn't sure. And right now he was too distracted to think about it. Someone was out to get him, and he had to find out who. "Up, up, and away," he said as he jumped out the door.

Crash!